The
Braintree Mission

THE MACMILLAN COMPANY
NEW YORK · CHICAGO
DALLAS · ATLANTA · SAN FRANCISCO
LONDON · MANILA

BRETT-MACMILLAN LTD.
TORONTO

The
Braintree Mission

A FICTIONAL NARRATIVE OF LONDON AND BOSTON
1770–1771

by
Nicholas E. Wyckoff

THE MACMILLAN COMPANY · NEW YORK
1957

FIRST PRINTING

PRINTED IN THE UNITED STATES OF AMERICA BY KINGSPORT PRESS, INC., KINGSPORT, TENNESSEE

Library of Congress catalog card number: 57-6353

Author's Foreword

THE NARRATIVE ENTITLED *The Braintree Mission* IS A WORK of fiction in a context of history. It concerns people, their patriotism and politics, in a period of time that has been well documented by historians, biographers, diarists, letter writers, pamphleteers, orators, and others. Historical events, and the characters and opinions of historical persons referred to in the tale, are presented with respect for accuracy.

The reader must be informed that two of the principal persons who appear in the narrative are entirely creations of fiction. They are Edward Humbird, sixth Earl of Hemynge, and Giuseppe Tompkins, his clerk. All episodes in which actual historical persons meet with these two, or consider their words or deeds, are of necessity fiction—in which, with equal necessity, there is a mingling of truth.

An even more controlling fictional element in the tale is the colonial policy attributed to Lord North's ministry in London in the year 1770. This policy, which motivates Lord Hemynge's mission to Boston, was never actually proposed. At odd times in the previous decade, various people both in England and in America gave ineffectual consideration to devices that in some ways resemble it. Of course, it ought to have been proposed, adopted, and effected with boldness. And if it had been, the results must have been almost precisely those set forth in the tale.

v

Quoted in the narrative are certain excerpts from the pleas submitted by John Adams and Josiah Quincy, Jr., in the Superior Court at Boston, in defense of the British soldiers charged with murder after the Boston Massacre. These are condensed from the reports of the trial contained in Frederic Kidder's centennial volume, *History of the Boston Massacre*, published by Joel Munsell, Albany, New York, 1870.

For the convenience of readers who may wish to have their memories refreshed informally as to certain persons who held chief responsibility for the policies of the British government of King, Lords, and Commons in the period dealt with here, a brief note on two prime ministers follows.

William Pitt the Elder, the "Great Commoner," was prime minister from 1757 to 1761. In this period he directed triumphantly England's widespread campaigns in the Seven Years' War (known as the last of the French and Indian Wars in North America). He resigned office in 1761 in disagreement with the young King George the Third, and also with his colleagues in the ministry.

Mr. Pitt was elevated to the peerage as first Earl of Chatham in 1766. In the same year he formed a ministry which he nominally headed but was unable to lead, after its first few weeks in office, owing to a complete collapse of health. He could not even summon the energy to resign until 1768. This curious leaderless administration is sometimes called the "Chatham ministry." Its chief never again held ministerial office, but continued to speak in the House of Lords, in opposition to the fatal American policies of Lord North's administration, to the very end of his life in 1778.

Lord North came to the fore as a Tory prime minister in January, 1770, when the Whigs were hopelessly divided and the King was determined upon having a friend in office. He was able in finance and in political manipulation, popular in the House of Commons, and certainly he was an endlessly loyal friend to the monarch—but he failed completely to grasp what was needed to conciliate the North American colonies. He held office, with the administration in power at the start of the tale, until 1782, after the loss of America to independence.

Part One

"WE MUST TAKE IT TO PITT," SAID LORD NORTH.

His visitor stared at him with an air of mild reproof.

"To Chatham, then," the King's First Minister conceded with a trace of annoyance.

His visitor smiled. "He must be informed, of course," he agreed. "But I have heard that he has suffered another attack lately. Perhaps we shall be taking it actually to Lady Hester."

Frederick North could exact payment in kind. It was his turn now to stare with a reproving coolness at his companion, Edward Humbird, Earl of Hemynge, who hastened to make the amends: "Oh—to the Countess of Chatham, by all means!"

There was a moment in which the two men could have given way to a fit of laughter. The impairment in popularity suffered by the great William Pitt since his elevation to the peerage still gave pleasure to various persons who held or sought high office. But the pleasure must remain fitful, for with Pitt no man could be certain that an eclipse would be total or lasting. He emerged, always, again so bright. On this occasion the mirth was restricted to an innocent movement of Lord Hemynge's eyelids and a slight pursing of Lord North's full lips. The business in hand was serious, and the prospect of consulting Pitt was even more so.

"The policy must be known to Chatham, or we shall be impotent to effect it," Lord North declared. "I do not expect opposition from him in this proposal. The conciliation of North America has been both a Pitt and a Chatham warhorse. The means proposed is new. Novelty is not likely to alienate *him*. And His Majesty has consented that Chatham shall be informed."

The Prime Minister did not consider it necessary to mention that the King's consent had been extremely reluctant, nor his own surprise that it had been given at all. His Majesty's readiness to be alienated by novelty was notorious.

Nor did Lord Hemynge need these disclosures to be impressed by his old friend's achievement. The new colonial policy that Lord North had just outlined to him in this midnight hour of secret conversation at Wroxton, the Minister's country seat, appeared to him simple, audacious, and magnificent. He was convinced that it must succeed. To have been sought out in his retirement to take part in effecting such a policy was an honor that pleased him deeply.

Frederick North's intrepidity amazed him. Certainly to have gone with this colonial policy to the King before sounding out Chatham, who fancied himself as such a benevolent patron to America, was reckless if not sublime. True, it was because Lord North had undertaken to go to the King first in all the affairs of state that he held the first office today. But managing the monarch was one thing, while managing the Parliament—and Chatham!—was another.

"You wager high on Chatham's consent, my lord," said the Earl of Hemynge.

"Yes—very high. And I shall win," declared Lord North.

When Lord Hemynge judged that praise was due, he was a man to speak it. "By God, I think you shall—and that you deserve to!"

Lord North had kissed hands and received the seals of the Treasury some five months ago, early in January of what already promised to be a difficult year—1770. He addressed Commons for the first time as chief of the government on the night

2

of March the fifth. On that occasion he had surprised many of his colleagues by his conciliatory tone toward the North American colonies. He had of course thrown a sop to the remnants of the Grenvillites and the Townshendites by suggesting that he expected some token of submission from Boston, for example. But the general purport of the outline of his colonial policy was "friendly," although he did not go to such extremes nor into such detail that any member of the House could have guessed what a radical measure the First Minister had in mind.

Then in April had come these ill news from the port of Boston in that most stubborn and refractory of all the colonies, the Massachusetts Bay. In the same night of March the fifth when Lord North had first faced the House of Commons with the King and his majority backing him, there had been an uprising of resistance to the royal arms then policing Boston. It was an occasion of violence which had been curbed only by the firing of a few rounds from the muskets of the troops of His Majesty's forces. Death had struck down some inconsequential persons in the street. Later despatches had reported a spirit of extreme unrest prevailing in Boston. It appeared that the affair had been dubbed by the townsfolk a "Bloody Massacre." What were King, Lords, and Commons to make of the intelligence that the Crown's appointed civil authorities there had required that the military commanders remove the troops from the town to an island fortress in the harbor? Was not this precisely an occasion upon which a Tory ministry must be expected to reverse a proposed policy of conciliation and to take up strong measures to restore order and compliance?

And must it not have appeared a final provocation that an officer and eight soldiers of His Majesty's forces were now reported to have been placed under arrest in Boston—by the civil authorities responsible to the Crown—on charges of *murder?* The best that those feeble bearers of the King's authority had been able to accomplish was postponement of the trial.

Yet in London, in the very face of these news, the leader

of the King's own party in the Parliament was secretly seeking support from the opposition, even from Chatham, for measures that went far beyond the ordinary meaning of the term "conciliation." Lord Hemynge found it mysterious and splendid that these were measures that urged no compulsion or punishment to be visited upon the colonial subjects, who could scarcely be seen as in anything less than a state of rebellion. On the contrary, they were measures that would change the complexion of the House of Lords itself, and would stir the passion of England's gentry as nothing since the seating of the Scottish peers had done in the days of Good Queen Anne.

The Earl of Hemynge faced the Minister. "And who, my lord, is to carry this proposal of Chatham?"

"You, Hemynge, and no one else," said Frederick North firmly to his dear old friend. "You have agreed to carry it to Boston. You shall take it to Chatham as well."

Edward Humbird, sixth Earl of Hemynge, stepped from his coach at Hayes Place in the high noon of a day early in May. The sunlight was clear and hot. There had been showers in the night and the park glistened now, its many shades of green seeming to throw off bright silver reflections.

Hester Grenville Pitt, Countess of Chatham, moved slowly across a terrace to greet him. She wore a yellow morning gown that hung too loosely on her tall ample frame, her hair under the most invisible of caps was in something of disarray, and she was unmistakably one of the strengths of the British Empire.

"You unannounced, Hemynge?" she called as she moved.

"And ripe with news for Chatham," he answered.

"Are they good or ill?" she demanded.

"How can I or any man say, Countess, till we observe how they are received by him?"

"If they are of India, he will relish them." Lady Hester was willing at least to offer some hope.

4

The Earl of Hemynge worshiped this lady, but he also was aware of the need to be firm with her. "No. They are of North America."

"Then they cannot be good," she declared mournfully. But it was rather comfortably that she went on: "Our appetite, when we have it these days, is all for news of East India—the spice trade, the silk trade, the imposts, the constables, the Company."

"Even without such news to secure my advantage with the Pitts, I must beg an audience. Is he fit to receive a communication from the King's First Minister?"

The Countess clearly intended to raise no obstacle. She touched Lord Hemynge's arm, and guided him gently toward the house. "The foot is elevated," she confided, "but not inflamed as it was two days ago. He imparted some Roman thoughts to our sons this morning."

Lord Hemynge was happy to learn that the future Earl of Chatham and William Pitt the Younger had heard something of Cato or Scipio this morning and, he hoped, not too much of Tarquin or Sulla. And privately he was as relieved as Chatham himself must be that the angrier phases of the present gout were abated.

Lady Hester led him through the hall of Hayes and up the broad staircase to the apartments at the front of the house. She left him in an anteroom for some ten minutes. Then she reappeared at the door to the inner chamber, summoning him.

An almost total darkness prevailed within the huge bed-chamber into which Lord Hemynge passed. A multitude of tapers in an elaborate brass candelabrum set on a tallboy was so screened as to throw its soft yellow illumination only upon a portrait of the Duke of Marlborough which hung above it—and upon the central figure in the room, the figure in the great stiff thronelike chair, the figure that dwarfed all other furniture and seemed to reduce the dimensions of the chamber itself. The figure gave an impression of stout bulkiness because it was wrapped so generously in fine soft flannels, velvet-bordered

5

coverlids, silken shawls—the latter of an India print, Lord Hemynge noted. High among the shawls was an aperture from which The Nose portended, a very Matterhorn among British— aye, among Scottish—noses. The leg was stretched forward, with the foot on a cushion that rested upon a stool. This extremity was partly concealed by filmy cloths draped across frames that might easily have been supposed to be hoops from a wine cask.

The Countess hovered near, as the visitor had known she would. She indicated by gesture that he was to seat himself upon a small stiff chair placed in the dimness so that its occupant must have a fine view of the central figure.

"Hemynge.—Sir, you are welcome."

Oh, the greeting was not enough to let The Voice sound forth, yet even so the tone that carried the brief formal syllables, muffled as it was among the shawls, had still enough of the familiar ring to set loose a small tremor compounded of chill and fire upon Edward Humbird's scalp.

He managed the only possible answer: "My lord."

"Call me by my name—call me Pitt."

Lord Hemynge smiled. "I shall be delighted to do so, my lord—Mr. Pitt!"

"Thank you," said The Voice. "What is your mission?"

"I hope, sir, and Lord North joins me in the hope, that you are making a good recovery. We wait for the day when you shall speak again in the Lords." He had almost said "House."

"I must be rid of these maladies," The Voice declared.

"There will be no opposition to that proposal, my lord." Lord Hemynge exhibited a despatch. "I bring you a letter from Lord North. He has appointed me to speak for him of a proposed policy touching conciliation of the North American colonies."

One of the shawls moved in such a fashion that it might be guessed that Lord Chatham was waving the letter aside. "Give it to Lady Hester," he said. His visitor did so. "What is the proposal, Hemynge?"

The envoy was prepared for the question. He desired to take

6

a deep breath before taking the plunge into his answer. But he managed an appearance almost of a man of wit uttering a piece of wit when he spoke.

"The proposal is to elevate several American colonial subjects to peerages, seat them in the Lords, and negotiate through them for the establishment of American boroughs with seats in the Commons. It is proposed to make the first selection for the peerages at once. The representation from North American boroughs in Commons must await the careful devising of a safe electoral system. The proposed policy acknowledges, with royal dignity and with no surrender of a decent firmness, some justice in the colonies' claim to representation before taxation."

Lord Hemynge paused. There was a quality of profoundly serious attention in the stillness with which the Earl and Countess of Chatham had heard his statement. Neither made a move to speak.

"Lord North's intent is to effectuate the policy with boldness, my lord. The North American peerages will not be offered to men of what may be called the 'Prerogative party' in America. They shall go to certain leaders of what may be called the 'Liberty party'—sometimes called the 'Patriots.' The Minister has appointed me to sail to Boston to sound out a number of persons there and to make a tentative selection, as a first trial. The proposed policy is of necessity to be kept secret and so must the negotiations in America be. Lord North has secured the consent of His Majesty and of Lord Bute. He has the consent of the Rockingham party, with Edmund Burke prepared to voice the support of the opposition in Commons."

Now at last there was a strong movement among the scarves, and William Pitt raised his arms to pluck aside the draperies that had concealed his countenance. His eyes blazed with the memory of great victories and bitter defeats—of deeds that had swept armies over Europe, fleets across the icy currents of Labrador; that had staked his beloved brother Wolfe to death on the Plains of Abraham, and raised a second beloved brother,

Jeffery Amherst, to vengeance and victory over the Bourbon. This was the face of the Great Commoner who had created an Empire fit for the enlightened and humane rule of the most inspired of Emperors and the most scrupulous of Senates, whose true sources of power should be derived from the minds and hearts of an imperial people, proud, loyal, and secure in their liberties. But the Emperor dealt out to Pitt and the people had been the third Hanoverian George; and the Senate that pretended to speak for the nation had been the Parliament that trafficked in general warrants, writs of assistance, stamp and excise taxes and, within its own lobbies, in a customary bribery. And then, nine years ago, at the summit of triumph, at the height of a dominion in government that had the passionate support of the English people whose liberties he revered, Great Britain's Greatest Commoner had been driven from his rightful place of ministry by a petulant prince who claimed to "glory in the name of Briton"—King George the Third.

It was true that five years later there had been his nominal leadership of a patchwork kind of ministry, a "coalition," shortly after William Pitt's elevation to the Earldom of Chatham. But those had been the years of his darkest eclipse, when his health had failed him utterly, his mind had been clouded, his energy and capacity had lain inert. Then the only person close to the ministry who had retained an unflawed loyalty to his leadership was his own Countess. "Government by Hester," of course, had offered opportunities to the opportunists both in and out of the administration. But for something over a year now he had been himself again: once more, as was proper, he rose in his place at Westminster to speak on the concerns of the Empire and the people; and the ministers as well as the Lords who heard him must consider their policies in the light of the positions he took.

Lord Hemynge could not but observe the face and listen for the words of such a man with a sense of awe upon him. How must William Pitt regard the present proposal to acknowledge the right of true-born Englishmen of the remote New

8

World to representation in the Parliament that claimed the constitutional power to legislate for them? Could he believe that the Parliament he had sought so tirelessly to educate was capable, after all, of learning some of the lessons in greatness he had tried to impart?

"So Lord North may do with the King's consent what I must have done at the proper time, years ago, but for the crossings of spite"—Lord Chatham's voice was reduced to a murmur, for he was addressing this thought to no other man than himself—"and should have done with hope of winning not merely these English consents, but with America's own consent. . . . With hope . . . with hope . . ." The voice trailed off into a whisper. Then its owner raised his head and faced his visitor with firm resolution spread upon his arrogant features. "The measure has a noble sound, my lord—and a tardy one. I have been accused of being mysterious on many occasions, but I am certain that I have never posed to any party or faction such a conundrum as this: Tell me, sir, how is it that such a motion comes to the minds of the noble lords in the ministry only now?"

Lord Hemynge had an answer for it. "Lord North in all humility acknowledges that the situation of the British Empire in North America is desperate, my lord. The proposal is offered as a desperate remedy for desperate ills."

Indignation as ever marked still more stiffly the lines of overpowering scorn in the fearsome Pitt countenance. "'A desperate remedy'? A desperate remedy, indeed, my lord!" cried Lord Chatham in the withering tone that could reduce the most heavily iron-clad, the most insensible members of Lords and Commons to trembling incompetence through hours of mortal debate. The Earl of Hemynge longed for company so that he need not serve as a lone target for this deadliest of fire. "That must indeed be 'a desperate measure' that would allow to three millions of free men their right to representation by elected persons of their own free choice—three millions of free Englishmen, at that! These are men who incline so little to bear oppression and tyranny that they fight like lions to rid themselves of the threat merely of being neighbor to a tyrannically ruled province, hundreds of miles remote from them across mountains, impenetrable forests, rivers like lakes, and lakes like seas. Do the noble lords forget that in the armies I sent forth to Canada under Loudoun and Abercrombie, Wolfe, Howe, and Amherst, fully a third of the troops were furnished by those proud and dauntless colonies of Great Britain? And the administration is willing *now* to take 'desperate measures' to recognize the constitutional right of such priceless, peerless Englishmen? Now, my lords?—*only* now? And 'desperate,' my lords? *How* 'desperate'?"

(Oh God, thought Lord Hemynge, is he with us or against us? And he even recalled Mr. Burke's phrase of denigration, "Chathamic fustian," as having a certain aptness.)

The trumpet solo went on. "Desperate? And a remedy? To offer as a first step toward representation an half-dozen of peers?" There was a full stop. Chatham was suddenly amazed. "And what peerages are these, my lord, that will accord to several lonely North Americans, seats in the House of Lords?"

Lord Hemynge was so grateful for the break that he was able to speak up with spirit. "The measure is generous, my lord," he said. "The peerages to be conferred are to be no less than earldoms. It is presumed the titles will be styled after North American territories or landholdings, as may suit the pleasure of the —ah, subjects concerned."

The information broadened the diversion. "Earldoms!" exclaimed Lord Chatham.

"Earldoms!" was a whispered echo from the Countess.

"No less, my lord," said Lord Hemynge with a touch of grim satisfaction. Like many Englishmen in the past three years, since the elevation of William Pitt, he suspected that earldoms might be a tender subject at Hayes. If so, so be it! he thought, with a flash of defiance.

As no comment was forthcoming, the envoy sought to prompt one. "This is handsome enough to be irresistible," he suggested.

10

"It is so handsome as to be monstrous!" exclaimed the Earl of Chatham.

In truth, he had no right to say so, thought Lord Hemynge. Many a true-born Englishman and many a continental European had judged that the Earldom of Chatham sat monstrously upon William Pitt. Chatham was not to England or Europe or America what Pitt had been, and he must know it. But from another, a more generous view, it must be a grudging Englishman indeed who would not admit that the Great Commoner had earned his coronet and ermine. He had, in fact, earned much more. And a reasonable man who knew the circumstances of his health and his fatigues must acknowledge, too, that while it might have become impossible for the man to manage the House of Commons any longer—the labors involved in that endless business being of a nature to require a faultless constitution—the direction of policy from a seat in the more restful House of Lords might yet be possible for him to undertake. That is, of course, if he should ever agree to form and head another ministry.

But Lord Chatham was summing, as though to himself, what he had heard. "Earldoms, to men of the Liberty party. North American peers to devise a system of borough representation for the colonies. North proposes. The King and the King's Friends consent. Rockingham consents." The great man frowned and threw a challenging look at his visitor.

"And my good brother Grenville?" he demanded.

Though he had hoped that William Pitt might not raise this question, chiefly out of consideration for Lady Hester's feelings for her brother, whatever they might be, Lord Hemynge was ready for it.

"Opposition to this policy is expected from the Gentle Shepherd of the Stamp Act, my lord," said the Earl of Hemynge.

Lord Chatham burst out laughing. The sound was rare from him, and Lady Hester looked upon him with an amazed and loyal delight.

Lord Hemynge was able to think gratefully that he had made

11

a hit. He had resorted basely to outright flattery, for the reference was to the occasion in Commons during the debate on a cider tax which had preceded the Stamp Act proposal, when George Grenville had been indignantly crying out to the House: "Will the gentlemen please tell me where else I can raise the money? Tell me where I can find an equal source of revenue? Tell me where . . ." And Pitt, sitting there placidly in the opposition benches, had begun to hum the measures of the popular song, "Gentle Shepherd, Tell Me Where," finally singing out that line as though in a rhapsody, while the entire House was convulsed with mirth. Then he had risen, bowed contemptuously, and stalked majestically from the chamber. It had been one of his greatest triumphs in the arts of devastation and demoralization. His brother Grenville had never lost the nickname of "Gentle Shepherd."

"You are astute, sir," cried Lord Chatham happily. "He will oppose."

"We are confident, my lord, that he will not carry the entire Bedford faction with him. In fact, we know that he will not."

"No, no," Lord Chatham agreed. "There are men of sense in that connection. But tell me, sir, how did you secure Mr. Burke's agreement? It is difficult for me to understand his consent, in view of his hatred of parliamentary reform."

"It was necessary to guarantee to him that the English boroughs would remain untouched in connection with this measure, my lord. This will not be offered as in any sense an *English* reform bill."

William Pitt was solemn again. "In a word, Mr. Burke accepts Boston on condition that Birmingham remain unrepresented?"

Lord Hemynge scented danger. "My lord, the time is overripe for a measure that may enable us to mend our relations with the North American colonies. The present proposal is offered as such a measure, and as nothing else."

The great statesman considered this. "The wounds of New England perhaps must be bound before we may medicate for such a chronic complaint, somewhat milder, as that perpetual Birmingham illness in our body politic," he conceded. "You

12

have won great consents to your proposal, my lord," he finally declared.

Lord Hemynge spoke quickly. "Great as these consents are, sir, they are nothing unless the Earl of Chatham does also consent."

"He does consent!" cried William Pitt, Earl of Chatham, with all those trumpets and trombones that were encased in his throat blaring forth a golden blast. Considerable portions of Lord Hemynge's skin responded to the sound with an eruption of goose flesh, and his scalp tingled.

"Then the policy must succeed, my lord." The visitor started to rise, supposing that the audience was ended.

"No, Hemynge—one moment." Lord Chatham raised his hand in an imperious holding gesture. "This policy must have succeeded ten, or as late as eight or six years ago, if proposed by an administration that our people in the colonies recognized as justly concerned for their interest. Today—I do not know. It may succeed or it may fail. In any case, it is certainly proposed very late. I cannot wish you well or ill in your mission. It may be that there is something more of 'this corruptible' in the men of the Liberty party in America than I have supposed. You and they shall determine it." He paused. "I shall await the result of your negotiation with curiosity, my lord."

"And I undertake it with curiosity—and with confidence, sir. Perhaps I may have the privilege of waiting upon you when I return?"

"Please do—I shall be impatient to hear from you."

The cue was unmistakable. Lord Hemynge rose and bowed. "Thank you, my lord. Good day—and good health to you."

Lord Chatham's dismissal was a bow of the head. Before his visitor turned away he was moving his hands mysteriously to restore the shawls to their function of veiling his countenance.

The Countess guided the visitor from the room, and summoned a servant to usher him from the house. Then she hurried back to the inner sanctum.

Standing a moment on the terrace, waiting for his coach,

Lord Hemynge was aware that he felt some fatigue from the interview just concluded. It was as though he had played a game of chess with a giant who moved his opponent's pieces for him, and who through some whim of mystification had permitted the game to end in a stalemate. But it was impossible to resent Pitt, if you really believed in his greatness as Edward Humbird did: Pitt was a real giant. As long as England had him, whether in his health or in his enfeeblement, she had what was essential to a great imperial power—a statesman who could see beyond the mazes and chafferings of imperial rulership to the people who composed the Empire and gave it whatever virtue it had. The comfort of having him at hand as a source of true British wisdom was far greater than the momentarily acute discomfort of consulting him.

Still, it was impossible to pretend that communication between giant and pigmy, with one's self perforce in the role of the pigmy, was an experience to be sought. Lord Hemynge entered his coach to leave Hayes Place with a strong sense of relief.

2

THE LENGTH OF THE VOYAGE MUST BE DETERMINED AS ALWAYS by the direction and force of the wind. The brig, H.M.S. *Cavalier,* left Bristol at mid-October before a fresh offshore breeze. Lord Hemynge hoped secretly that the vessel might encounter a calm in midpassage. The many interviews he had had with persons acquainted with colonial policy and affairs had made him a very full man. The informations he had acquired filled many despatch cases, letters, and journals. The envoy's sense of the need to review and digest this matter was rather casual—but it did exist.

More immediate was his sense of desire for an extended period of leisure. The extreme pressure of business he had suffered in the months since he had agreed to undertake a delicate mission at the request of his old friend, Frederick North, was more than he had bargained for.

Edward Humbird had retired from an active naval command in the year 1750, when the death of his brother, the fifth earl, had brought about his succession to the coronet. Then in his middle thirties, he had begun with zeal and industry the task of bringing the great properties of Hemmingcourt into good repair. He had also contracted a marriage with the Lady Dorothy Cranbrough, that firm-handed horsewoman out of the Northumberland hills and marshes. The successive births

15

of two sons within two years had provided the usual number of heirs to the Humbird line, and the partners to the marriage thereafter consorted only rarely. The Countess divided her year between Bath and the Scottish border, and the Earl moved between Humbird House in London and the seat at Hemming-court.

But the greatest influence on Lord Hemynge's pursuits ashore stemmed from an acquaintance he had formed with Mr. Handel during the last years of the great musician's life. An admiration for the infinite capacity and undimmed courage of that imperious man as blindness grew upon him drew the peer's interest toward his music. The curious inquiry quickly developed in him a passion. Lord Hemynge opened his London house to what his Admiralty friends designated "a rabble of fiddlers, tinklers, and balladmongers." But he found that he enjoyed the company of musicians above all other company, and with the stubbornness of a man trained in the Royal Navy he adopted this "rabble" as his own. His older acquaintances from the circles of the seagoing and the fashionable who wished to retain intercourse with him were forced to acquire impressive capacities for listening. Some of them, in this unaccustomed practice, developed ears and willingness to use them. The society that with the passing of years came to Humbird House on Thursdays for rehearsal of the tunes in old manuscripts of Mr. Purcell and in forgotten commissions filled in haste by Mr. Handel, as well as of much odd musical scribbling brought in from Rome and Paris, took on gradually a character that was sometimes designated as "The Faithful."

The sixth Earl himself proved his own faith with works by submitting to instruction in harpsichord playing, and to the endless repetitions of practice necessary to advancement in this skill. It was not unjust that in some of the letters exchanged among The Faithful he should be named "Il Pastor Fido." This was the name also of a masque of Mr. Handel's—which, incidentally, was performed with an especial success at Humbird House in April of 1766, a few weeks after royal assent was given to the act of Parliament repealing George Grenville's Stamp Act.

As a result of his pains, Lord Hemynge became in time a fairly comfortable performer at the harpsichord, one able with coaching to supply a very modest elaboration of the ground bass in a *concerto grosso* or a *sonata da camera*.

This patron to music was understood to be too fully occupied to be able to give much time to attendance upon debates in the House of Lords. Nevertheless, he was far from a forgotten peer. The fact is that he had left the Admiralty owning a not inconsiderable reputation as an officer with a capacity for negotiation. He was called on occasionally by ministers in various governments to serve as an envoy in missions that required a certain delicacy in the accomplishment. On such occasions, Lord Hemynge's freedom from commitment to any party or, as Chatham called it, faction, was an advantage.

A story out of his seagoing days that somehow did not die down around the dining tables at Hayes and Stowe, Beaconsfield and Wroxton, reminded gentlemen who were close to the secretaryships of state that the Earl of Hemynge was a likely man for such-and-such a piece of business.

Once while he was serving as captain in the Mediterranean Fleet Admiral's flagship, a mutinous midshipman had escaped from the vessel in harbor at a port on the island of Cyprus, and was concealed by the inhabitants of the town. The angry Admiral's threats of siege and cannonading had no effect on the islanders. These were empty threats, and the Cypriots knew it. When the Admiral ordered Captain Humbird to secure the fugitive or suffer unpleasant consequences, the young officer promptly invited the ladies of the local chieftain's court to go a short cruise aboard the vessel. In the evening of that day, after the ladies were returned to shore, the mutineer was quietly given over to the Admiral.

This story had been freshly recounted to Lord North at Wroxton a few weeks before he had settled on his new departure in colonial policy. The minister had not been heard to comment

17

on the tale. But it was known to his intimates that he was familiar with it, and his subsequent action in assigning Lord Hemynge to conduct a certain piece of business was understood to signify that it was not displeasing to him.

❦

For several reasons the date of the envoy's departure for the Massachusetts Bay was subjected to a series of postponements. First, there were the rumors that began to get about London shortly after Lord Hemynge's visit to Hayes. It was believed that if nothing whatsoever were done for a time, these whispers to the effect that Lords North and Chatham and others were forming a cabal against the King, to the end that a score of Virginia, New York, Pennsylvania, and Carolina Tories were to be awarded baronetcies and admitted to a new kind of House of Petty Colonial Lords at Philadelphia (all as a punishment to the Massachusetts Bay radicals) might die down—as indeed they did. Then it was considered that the envoy should be well advised to wait till after the trials of the officer and the troopers that were to be held in the Superior Court at Boston. But the Bostonians postponed the trials so many months that in the end this consideration had to be abandoned.

The Earl of Hemynge, during these protracted periods of waiting, devoted a good deal of time to study of conditions in the Massachusetts, from such sources as were at hand in London. He read, for example, a history of the province written by one Thomas Hutchinson, and was horrified by the account of the privations to which those people dubbed "puritans" had voluntarily submitted themselves.

In other hours he took the trouble to wait upon a number of persons who had had some experience of royal or other service to the province, among them three former royal governors. He was not permitted to disclose to these nor to anyone else the nature of his mission, and submitted to them only that he had been appointed by Lord North to make some observations on colonial affairs in North America, with the object of settling some of the costly differences currently agitating relations.

Among these Sir William Shirley was the most garrulous and the least helpful. The old gentleman had lately passed his seventy-fifth birthday, was of a twinkling humor, and carried about him the remains of a rather grand military manner. He had been recalled from Boston some fifteen years earlier, and presently was Governor of the Bahamas, enjoying a summer's visit in England. These seemed pleasant enough responsibilities and circumstances to keep an old man fairly happy, but it appeared that there was something about the Massachusetts Bay colony that haunted those who had ever held any authority in her affairs.

Sir William, with something of apology and self-justification, insisted to Lord Hemynge that he had once had great hopes of the Boston men—"very good soldiery they would have made, sir"—whose militia he had led in that first unfortunate expedition against the French at Niagara in 1755. While it could not be denied that Sir William himself had led that ill-fated campaign, the cause of its failure somehow must be attributed to the ministry, then under the timid guidance of the Duke of Newcastle. Lord Hemynge found this not implausible, as so many disasters had flowered under the administration of Mr. Pitt's predecessor as chief of the government, that the French themselves might be willing to credit some of their more obscure victories to Newcastle.

Sir William announced his intention to return to the Massachusetts to live out his years of retirement; but of recent events there he had little information. He had known some of the Bostonian leaders mentioned in the reports of the shocking events—Tom Hutchinson, of course, and the Olivers. That very solid man, the elder Hancock, and the Quincy connection—fine gentlemen, certainly. But take these Adamses, now—he didn't seem to recall the name. "Where the devil did this brace of Adamses come from?" If the question was one that a former governor of the colony could not answer, Lord Hemynge had no intention of trying to answer it for him.

The suspended envoy found another former royal governor, Thomas Pownall, very full of business as secretary to the Board of Trade. This gentleman's administration in Boston, following immediately upon Sir William Shirley's, had been popular with the province. It had been during the French wars and he had been conspicuously helpful to Major General Amherst. Mr. Pownall had gained credit, no doubt, from the amazing triumphs of that commander for William Pitt. He had, moreover, harbored amiable sentiments toward the Massachusetts and North America at large, and evidently continued to do so; for he assured Lord Hemynge that his every waking moment was fully engaged in the interest of the Grand Ohio Company for the development of profitable new western colonies. He received the information that the peer was appointed to visit America most warmly, if briefly. Oh, yes, he had confidence in the future of America. On Lord Hemynge's return from Boston, Mr. Pownall was certain, he would be filled with the desire to invest something more tangible than confidence in the Northwest. He had stated his position long ago: seats in the British Parliament alone would quiet the American unrest. Lord Chatham was right—in *everything*. Recent and present ministries must accept blame. Certainly they had not heeded his—Thomas Pownall's—advice. . . .

Sir Francis Bernard, the latest of the royal governors at Boston, who had been recalled within the past year, was actually a person to whom Lord Hemynge might have taken something of a fancy. The peer waited upon Sir Francis in apartments near St. James' Park, and took an immediate interest in the light and pleasant decoration, the furnishings, the pictures, and the books with which the retired colonial patron of architecture had surrounded himself. But the baronet's temper belied his genial appearance. The recall from Boston by a craven ministry still burned him with shame; his mind was divided between a desire for revenge upon the Boston patriots—the "Bastards of Liberty . . . for that's what they are, my lord, not 'Sons,' as they style themselves, not in any degree true 'Sons'"—and a desire to denounce, censure, and humiliate the Whigs, scattered and beaten though they were by Lord North's ascendancy.

Never before had any civil magistrate suffered such perverse betrayals by his principals as he, Sir Francis, had suffered as governor in Boston from the hands of the late despised "speckled" ministry in London. True, they had sent him troops at last, two years ago, when the colony had reached a state of rebellion and lawlessness that threatened all order, all decency, all property, all constituted and chartered authority. But they had so tied his hands as to the use of the troops that neither he nor General Gage had been able to settle anything before he was recalled to London—apparently upon the petitioning of the rebel faction itself—which, of course, had dominated the Boston Town Meeting, and which had in the end dominated the Legislature, the General Court.

"I understand, my lord," Sir Francis complained, quite short of breath, "that Lord North is calling the regiments he sent over to me the 'Adams regiments'! Is not this a wicked levity, sir? We sentenced Admiral Byng to be shot, on most uncertain evidence of cowardice, some dozen years ago. Today we order our troops to behave as cowards, to 'give no cause of offense' to a rioting populace—and we issue that order in the name of the British Parliament.

"I wonder, my dear sir, that the government has the effrontery to ask you to visit Boston. Do they give you a safe-conduct? Do they send you escorted? Do they warn you that an emissary from the ministry at London is sure to be received as a laughingstock, a butt, in Boston? Oh, my lord, we are come upon evil days, that the might of England trembles before the petty wrath of a colonial seaport!"

21

Lord Hemynge did not identify himself closely with party, but was inclined to be Whiggish and a follower of Pitt. He did not permit himself to be overcome by the rather impressive wrath of an outraged colonial governor, who was clearly Tory. He determined to ask a question. It might draw more wrath, but surely he was gaining no intelligence from the governor's present vein.

"These Boston patriots, sir—is it possible they are encouraged in their defiance by the French?"

"No, it is not possible," exploded Sir Francis. "The cowards have been as afraid of the French as our ministers have been—since Pitt."

"Then what is the source of this disaffection?" the peer calmly inquired.

"It is an unique, a peculiar Boston devilry," the magistrate whose seat had lately been at Boston replied. "It is fomented by some half-dozen of shameless, perverse, traitorous propagandists. The galleys are too good for 'em."

"But is there no suitable treatment in reserve for 'em?" his lordship asked.

"Hanging!" shouted Sir Francis. "It will come to that, Hemynge—it must: Adams, the palsied brewer; Hancock, the smuggler; Otis, the mad lawyer—his pupil, the other Adams. It doesn't matter who we hang. It's the only measure that will tell 'em where we stand." Then the baronet, spent of his passion, recalled an alternative. "If they don't force us to hang half a dozen of our own soldiers first. Our only hope is poor Tom Hutchinson. He, sure, is the best subject they have produced from the native soil over there. He was my lieutenant-governor —and I made him Chief Justice of the province on his own merits. He is a man of some genius in the arts of government. I brought him along a bit, and they hate him now worse than they do me. They could get the ministry to call me home, but Tom belongs there. He's one of 'em. It just may be that through him, we can set them back yet. It may be he's shrewd in postponing this trial of our soldiers. I'd go far in backing Hutchinson. He's my man." Sir Francis turned gravely to his visitor. "I'm sure you'll find him yours, too, my lord, as soon as you've set foot in Boston."

"He's not the historian?" Lord Hemynge queried.

Sir Francis warmed noticeably. "He is, indeed, my lord. Their best and, so far as I know, their sole historian. The provincials yonder profess to hold his work in high esteem. But when they sacked his house five years ago in the Stamp Act agitation, they destroyed, along with the rest of his property in the town, the manuscripts and notes of a later volume of this same history. Oh, not quite destroyed"—the baronet corrected himself—"for the manuscript was discovered the next morning lying mud-soaked in the street."

"A fortunate survival," Lord Hemynge conceded. "And do the man's sentiments as a patriot survive also?"

"Hutchinson is a patriot of the British Empire, devoted wisely to the true interest of the Massachusetts Bay province of which he is native," Sir Francis explained with an air of pride in his protégé. "I should not apply to him the term 'patriot' in the sense that it has acquired in Boston. That honorable word has been corrupted over there by the 'Give-us-liberty-and-license' party of rebels and rioters." The baronet reflected a moment. "I hope—I still dare to hope that the ministry will undertake to be wise, and will appoint him to the royal governorship to succeed me. I must believe that your own observations in Boston shall weight your opinion in favor of the appointment, my lord."

Lord Hemynge would commit himself only to the hope that he might have the honor of making Mr. Hutchinson's acquaintance in Boston—for the baronet's description of Thomas Hutchinson's relation to the Patriot party suggested that this esteemed native of the province was not eligible to be considered for the contemplated honors he was empowered to offer—or at least to dangle.

23

From these agents of Hanoverian government of the fractious province Lord Hemynge turned with curiosity to an interview with Dr. Franklin, long a resident in London, and recently appointed as agent there for the House of Representatives of the Massachusetts Bay General Court. The learned doctor perceived quickly that the peer did not intend to disclose the nature of his projected business in Boston, and accordingly took refuge in an ignorance that he could quite logically claim.

It was some years since he had visited Boston. . . . He was greatly honored by the appointment conferred upon him lately by the lower house of the provincial legislature . . . but his being stationed in England—blessed land!—had prevented his enjoying the advantage of conversation with his principals since then. He was aware of the urgency of the grievances suffered by the people of the province, and especially of the town, as the result of the tragic affair of March the fifth . . . but he had no more information actually than Lord Hemynge himself might have acquired from the distressing accounts in the pamphlets and depositions that had been printed on order of the Town Meeting, and signed by James Bowdoin for the Committee of the Town.

It was true that Lord Hemynge had these publications (and other communications expressing a markedly different point of view) from the hand of the Earl of Hillsborough, in fact. But even though the agent would not speak out on the matter, Lord Hemynge found his conversation engaging. From stories of Dr. Franklin's early life in the Massachusetts, they turned to talk of sea voyages and of fishing and swimming. The peer recollected the philosopher's remarks on cannibalism among deep-sea fish as especially amusing. Dr. Franklin had pursued the subject to point out certain traits of the fish in mankind.

"I once knew a young man who had two narrow apertures in the neck, so placed that they should have served him excellently as gills," the American philosopher asserted. "We took swimming baths together with some frequency in various Pennsylvania waters. He was not more than a middling swimmer. I could always paddle faster and farther than he. But I always felt it should have been the opposite case. —I am sorry to tell you that the young man's life was ended by drowning. My own has not yet ended in that fashion."

Feeling somewhat wearied after a series of such interviews, Lord Hemynge retreated to Bath for a course of the waters. The sensation of the season at that resort was the presence of John Wilkes, Esquire, who had repaired there on his release from the King's Bench prison at St. George's Fields, after serving twenty-two months of a sentence imposed on him for printing blasphemous and seditious libels. A duly elected member of the House of Commons for the County of Middlesex, he had been expelled from Parliament on the insistence of the King, but had promptly been re-elected by his constituents while he was imprisoned. Debate on a second motion to expel him had brought the formidable Lord Chatham back to the Lords for one of his most persistent defenses of civil rights, and of the people's right to free election of representatives of their own choice. Chatham, while declaring he felt no liking for John Wilkes' person or morals, rose to speak no less than forty-five times during the endless debates on this member's expulsion.

Lord Hemynge was struck by the calmness of the Stormy Petrel's demeanor when he met him at the Pump one morning. He greeted the expelled member with interest.

"I am glad to see, sir, that you have not been deprived of health and spirits while deprived of your liberty."

"Thank you, my lord," said Mr. Wilkes, who knew that the Earl of Hemynge had made one of his rare attendances upon the Lords to vote for the Chatham amendment that would have restored his rights—an amendment defeated by a vote of eighty-nine to forty-three. "Health and spirits are not subject to parliamentary resolutions. I do not believe that liberty can long remain subject to parliamentary corruption. I received a steady stream of gifts and testimonials from persons in both

25

high and modest place during my confinement. Some of the most liberal of these were from our fellow citizens in North America, I must tell you."

Lord Hemynge's curiosity became intense. "Which provinces were so moved, may I ask?"

"From Charleston in the Carolina came the most handsome gift of all—some fifteen hundred pounds."

The peer caught his breath before he could pursue his point. "And I must suppose that Boston in the Massachusetts Bay was heard from, also?"

Mr. Wilkes' sallow, squinting countenance wrinkled with a smile. "Ah, Boston!" he exclaimed. "It is from that stout seaport that our Tory ministers must learn their sharpest lessons in the art of governing true-born Englishmen, faithful to the liberties of us all. Yes, my lord, I have heard from Boston. The commerce and prosperity of the town have been so dissipated by King, Lords, and Commons that Boston has little store from which to make gifts these days. But from her true Sons of Liberty I have only now received a fairly animated remembrance." He paused, savoring his own enjoyment of the tribute. "They have sent me two very large live turtles. Their names, I understand, are 'Wilkes' and 'Liberty.' Their persistence in surviving hazards and catastrophes is said to be endless. I am told it is practically impossible to kill 'em!"

Mr. Wilkes gave Lord Hemynge a look in which there was an odd mixture of the triumphant and the sardonic. As it did so often in these days since he had become responsive to music, the Earl's scalp tingled. The sensation, indeed, was his most reliable guide to "the right note."

The failure of the intelligence he had been able to gather in England to show much consequence was not especially disappointing to Lord Hemynge. He was a man who was inclined to trust the evidence taken in by his own eyes, a mariner's eyes; and by his own ears, lately become a musician's ears—rather han that reported to him by others. There was one person only who, in these late middle years of the Earl's life, might claim to have his confidence as an observer and reporter. That was his secretary, Giuseppe Tompkins, who deserves a note in the history of this mission, even though his part in it be minor.

Tompkins had been shipped off to Boston in May with no other orders than to keep his little eye open and to keep his rather large ear inclined to whatever he might hear. Lord Hemynge had advised him to regard his visit to the Massachusetts Bay as part of a belated Grand Tour. But the peer had seen to it that Tompkins read the pamphlet descriptive of what the colonial committee called the "horrid massacre" of March the fifth, and that his servant was aware that the mission to America was somehow involved with that affair. With no more specific orders than these, Tompkins could be trusted to apply his senses, sharpened in the streets of London, to observation of men and opportunities in the restive American seaport.

This personal attendant—a man now of some thirty years in age—had been a part of Edward Humbird's household for fteen years. The son of a London woman who had been seduced by an Italian bass singer in Mr. Buononcini's opera company in 1740, the nameless creature had had to fend for imself in London's darker alleys through a boyhood ever near to starvation. He had never made any acquaintance with the talian side of his parentage and had learned to speak only the urest speech of Bow Bells. Between the ages of fifteen and hirty—during his attendance upon Lord Hemynge—his appearance had changed little. He was then as now big-eared nd big-eyed, excessively bony, and somehow overscored by a stiff-curled mop of black hair that resisted any restraint xcept that of the soft broad-brimmed black hat he wore n the street. With his headgear, indeed, he was expressive, or with simple twists of the crown and brim he could give is hat a variety of styles—the swaggering, the rustic, the inister, even the elegant—that would have done credit to Mr. Garrick's hatter in Drury Lane.

If Tompkins in these years of comfortable attachment to an

opulent house confined the light touch of his fingers to such a detail of costume, in his boyhood their facility had helped to keep him alive. The crucial act of his youth was the lifting of a fife from one of a strolling band of musicians at the gates of Vauxhall when he was twelve years old. He had then proceeded to instruct himself in the art of playing tunes on the instrument. His grotesque variations in Covent Garden one day drew the notice of Andrew Dubourg, a musical familiar of Lord Hemynge. Mr. Dubourg befriended the boy, took him into his house as a lackey, and amused himself by teaching the cheeky little fellow to play upon the flageolet, and finally the hautboy. Young Tom was quick to absorb instruction in letters and notes, too. In time he became one of the best copyists of musical manuscript in London.

Mr. Dubourg on a few occasions entrusted the youth with wind parts in musical pieces performed at Humbird House. The Earl's interest, which must have been engaged by anyone with Tom's operatic ancestry, was benevolent toward the boy.

In the year 1755 Lord Hemynge was stricken with illness, a putrid throat, and suffered a long confinement. To divert him Mr. Dubourg had proposed that the boy Giuseppe Tompkins serve him as a reader, in particular of English poetry. The creature's performance in rendering aloud the edifying couplet was so toweringly strange and fantastic as to exercise a spell of profound bewitchment upon the mind of the languid invalid.

On his recovery the Earl had persistently sued Mr. Dubourg for permission to acquire the services of Tompkins in his own establishment. In the end, the lad entered Lord Hemynge's retinue. Trained as amanuensis and as keeper of the Humbird collection of music manuscripts, Tompkins became indispensable to the peer. It may also be said that the manner of living practiced at Humbird House and Hemmingcourt became indispensable to Tompkins.

It was understood that in his present exploratory mission to Boston, Tompkins was not to commit his observations to letter. In spite of this prohibition—a wise one, for letters between

28

subjects of the Crown in Great Britain and in her colonies were
very apt to be intercepted these days, and to be read aloud
before the Mother of Parliaments or colonial legislatures by
malicious persons interested in stirring dissension—the same
sloop that had carried Tompkins westward in May returned in
July with a screed for the Earl from his secretary's hand.

" 'Tis with the Deepest Vanity of Regrets, My Lord," the letter set forth, "that I must convey Intelligence of the condition of
Your humble servant to Your Lordship. In sum, Sir, 'tis that I
am compelled to live out the remainder of my days, whatever
my mortal Span may prove to be, upon this distant Tropical
shore. It doth appear that my frame will never survive another
Illness such as passage across the Wide Sea do impose upon it.
Tis beyond thinking that I should ever submit myself again,
with all Reverence due Your Gracious Lordship, to such a Torment of the Vomits. Your Lordship's Masterful Self hath served
the Admiralty in His Majesty's ships, moving freely from one
Sea to another, retaining in Your Lordship's gracious Stomach
such sustenance as it befits Your high Discretion, Sir, to put
here. From Your humble and faithful servant, Dear My Lord,
such means of keeping alive at Sea is denied with savage
Violence, as of Volcanoes. . . . Mayhap in Your Kind Graciousness, Your Lordship may designate a fitting service for me in
these provinces where life as though in the Barrens of Africka
doth stretch before me like a Desert. Indeed, My Dear Patron, it
is a most dismal prospect before me that I am thus compelled to
live out my days in a place that, upon my word, I do Detest.
But travel across a sea again, that, Dear Sir, I cannot contemplate. . . ."

Lord Hemynge laughed upon reading this complaint, but he
put himself to the trouble of writing a letter in reply and dis-
patched it promptly to Tompkins in the American desert. He
assured his trusted servant that his return passage to Great
Britain would be made in the company of his patron in a ship
of sufficient weight to be notable for steadiness. He also in a
guarded paragraph reminded Tompkins that of all the tidings

arriving from the Massachusetts Bay those concerned with the coming trial of the British soldiers connected with the affray of March the fifth were of greatest concern to his master. "I anticipate hearing from you some truly 'American' views of these matters when I arrive on that desert shore and regain your estimable advices."

Besides the volume of despatches and pamphlets he had with him in his cabin aft in the brig *Cavalier*, Lord Hemynge had brought along a packet of manuscripts of music. It was to these that he turned in weary hours as storms and heavy skies isolated the ship in a tossing universe. He read them over and over, sang the airs to himself, and sometimes cursed himself for a fool ever to have left the nobly spacious and warmly illuminated libraries of Hemmingcourt and Humbird House.

∽

Weather so delayed H.M.S. *Cavalier* in her passage that the master put her into the Newfoundland harbor at St. John's during a week late in November. Lord Hemynge went ashore and submitted to crude entertainment in the bleak stockade that passed for a customs headquarters on the fisherman' island. It was during the first week of December that the brig moved before stormy winds down the coast of Nova Scotia to the Massachusetts Bay. She entered the harbor of Boston toward dusk of a Sunday evening, and was piloted to an anchorage off Castle William. She was enveloped there in mists that impressed Lord Hemynge as the most cheerless, most dank and most penetratingly chill vapors that had ever smothered a quarter-deck upon which he stood. Wrapped in a heavy surtout he had found useful in his cruises of the Baltic Sea some twenty-five years earlier, his lordship wore also an air of patience; but in truth he felt a considerable dismay at the prospect of spending one more night aboard the frosted and salt crusted ship.

Boston, whatever else might be said of it as a seat of trouble, was a provincial capital among whose edifices there must surely be some decent hearths before which a man might stand with his back to the fire, warming his legs and his buttocks and his hands.

As the peer was about to turn away from the rail to go below, he saw a faint golden gleam moving through the mist, toward the ship. It held his eye and stopped his breath with a sudden hope. For it was a boat—beyond doubt it was a boat, her way lighted by a torch held by a man in her bow. Then there were the hails.

From the boat: "Who are you?"

From the ship: "Brig *Cavalier*, Admiralty, London. What boat is that?"

"From Castle William."

The boat glided closer. An officer standing behind the torchbearer gave an order to the two oarsmen, and hailed again: "Is the Earl of Hemynge aboard?"

The captain answered. "He is aboard. Come alongside."

A ladder was dropped and the officer climbed aboard easily. "Lieutenant Minchin, 14th Regiment. With the compliments of Lieutenant Colonel William Dalrymple, commanding."

The captain and the peer acknowledged the salute.

The young officer went on. "I am sent to inform his lordship that the Lieutenant Governor, Mr. Hutchinson, and Colonel Dalrymple have arranged quarters at Castle William for him this night. The boat alongside is provided to convey his lordship to the shore."

The master of the vessel sent sailors below to fetch portmanteaus and a trunk from Lord Hemynge's cabin. Presently the peer and his impedimenta were in the boat, moving across still water to an island shore that was completely invisible.

3

LORD HEMYNGE ACCEPTED CASUALLY THE REGIMENTAL COURTE-
sies with which he was received, but kept a corner of his eye,
in which sat a beam of amusement, on Tompkins. The creature
hung back discreetly through the ceremony of welcome at the
landing stage, hovering all modestly until the peer was ushered
to the unused chamber that was kept in order for General Gage.

His lordship and his faithful servant were alone at last in the
General's quarters about nine in the evening. The chamber was
furnished in a style rather more spare than Lord Hemynge had
hoped when he gave in momentarily on the deck of the
weather-beaten vessel to the desire for the warmest comforts
Boston hospitality might afford a weary traveler. But it did
contain a hearth, and a fairly comfortable blaze drew him to
stand as he had pictured himself doing, toasting his nether
limbs from the rear.

"Come now, Tom," said the peer, "how did you manage all
this?"

"All what, milud?" Tompkins inquired innocently.

"All this welcoming business, supper with the Colonel, stow-
ing away in the General's quarters—even that boat out to ferry
me in, timed to the minute. It's as though I should be the new
Governor come to succeed Sir Francis Bernard and put what's-
his-name—Hutchinson out of countenance."

"'Tis certain they could do no less, milud," Tom insisted

pompously. Then a Bostonian thought struck him. "Perhaps you do come as the new Royal Governor, God Bless Y'r Excellency, and there'll be more than a few to cheer you in when you take over from Stingy Tommy!"

Lord Hemynge was shocked. "No, Tompkins, that's too much. Hutchinson—it's *Thomas* Hutchinson, isn't it? They really can't put that name to him?"

"Oh, they put it to him right handily along Ship Street over in the town, milud." Tompkins showed a trace of relish.

"I'm sad to hear it," the peer said with what appeared to be a genuine regret, for it was sometimes in his mood to wish men in high place as fair a freedom from the scurrilous epithet as possible. (He had particularly hated the application of "Lady Cheat'em" to Hester Grenville Pitt in the early days of the Commoner's elevation.) "I daresay you've been harassing and prompting all these people to receive me properly. But tell me, dear boy, how did you know that the brig would make anchorage tonight? Have you worked out a conspiracy with messenger pigeons or gulls in some sort?"

"To be quite open with you, milud, 'tis my friends in the fishing trade, off the Grand Banks, brought in posts on the progress of the brig."

"Oh," said his lordship, "so the maritime news are carried by dolphins!"

"Not quite, sir," Tom corrected him. "I have had some fish-masters on the lookout for the brig the past fortnight. They potted her in Newfoundland waters, and the word was passed along. The fishing smacks is faster than you would believe, milud. They bob about something bloody, and they do say it is common for the oldest hands to suffer the sea sickness."

"The very malady that attacked you on the voyage from Bristol, eh!"

Tompkins shuddered. "May we pass over that, by your leave, milud?"

"Of course, dear boy," said his patron. "But I am sure that when we return together in what I most firmly hope shall be a larger vessel, there will be a seaworthiness grow upon your own members as it is proved in the timbers of the vessel herself. And in any case it shall be both my duty and my pleasure to minister to you. Let us never forget, Tom, that your first service to me was during a malady of my own. It is only just that the service should be repaid—in reverse."

Tompkins appeared to have a distaste for the word "reverse" in this connection, but was able to mutter: "Since it is your ludship's pleasure, quite so, milud."

Lord Hemynge looked at him searchingly for a moment.

"What have you to tell me about the state of affairs in Boston, Tom?" he demanded. Then he added, with emphasis: *"In brief."*

Tompkins' composure wavered, as it always did when the Earl called with firmness for brevity. The happy line, for him, was the one that might be amply developed, with variations, digressions, and counterpoint. But the devoted secretary in him now faced the hard challenge to be concise. Tom usually took a slight revenge at such a point by infusing an element of the cryptic into his response.

"The town of Boston is much more calm than you might expect, milud—on the surface. But there is reason to believe that this be the calm between two storms, like. There is the storm of March the fifth. And there may be the storm that breaks when sentence is passed on the poor soldiers that was trapped into that affair—the Bloody Massacre, it's called hereabouts. You have reached Boston in time to hear the defense in the court tomorrow. I commend the courtroom to your attention, milud. It will tell you more than I can."

"Come now, Tom," said his lordship, "you've been here nearly half a year. I expect more from you than a formal wave toward the King's Bench. How has the town taken to you, for example?"

"In my character, sir, as a Wilkes man—"

"Yes, I'm sure you're more Wilkite than Johnny Wilkes himself. By the way, do you know anything about two Bostonian turtles named 'Wilkes' and 'Liberty'?"

"Oh, milud!" Tom protested piously.

"I see that you do," the Earl asserted firmly. "That may have been a rather neat piece of business. Well, go on. What about this Wilkite character of yours?"

"In truth, milud," a slightly chastened Tompkins began, "the character do go down pretty well with the Sons o' Liberty party. Many's the evening I've passed with 'em in the clubs—various lodgings, taverns, and such, with the ale and the cider and the tobacco pipes. They made me free o' the Town Meeting. They march me in the parades near the barracks, milud, and I've played the winds for 'em many an evening a-serenading ladies of some of these gentry you'll be seeing in the courtroom tomorrow, milud."

"I'm glad you've kept in practice," said the peer thoughtfully. "Eh, so the gentry crowd the gallery here for this show, just as they did in Commons when the King's Friends were out to unseat poor old Johnny Wilkes!"

"They'll be on hand, milud," Tom declared sagely. "Quincys, Otises, Warrens, Bowdoins, Sewalls, Hancocks, Thayers, Adamses. They must hear the end of the sad, sad story."

"Yes? For whom is all this sadness in store? The soldiers? Or their enemies?"

"That, milud," Tompkins set forth owlishly, "is for you to witness with your own eyes in court tomorrow."

Lord Hemynge threw a glance of indulgent disgust toward his faithful servant. Then he tried a new attack. "Just how are these Adamses embroiled in all this business, Tom? I notice you slurred over the name when you spoke of the townsfolk I am to see sitting like anti-Wilkites in the gallery tomorrow. They were jeering in London at the regiments here as the 'Adams Regiments' before I left, you know. Old Governor Shirley was baffled by the name. What am I to expect of them? Who are they?"

35

Tom's eyelids fluttered as he prayed for strength to maintain his policy of mystification. It was so tempting a chance to go ahead full torrent on these subjects. But he knew his master. Lord Hemynge could be drawn much further in such a mood if he were kept in suspense.

"One, milud, is the town clerk of Boston. The Sons o' Liberty watches him right close for his winks and blinks and nods. He bears a sad affliction, milud—the palsy. And he be called Sam. T'other be John, a man o' law. Him you shall hear in the court tomorrow, sir, in defense of the poor soldiers. Yet after he announced he was for the defense, sir, he be elected by Town Meeting to sit in the Assembly of the General Court for Boston —that being, as you know, sir, Commons in a small way, so to speak."

"And are these brothers—"

"Not brothers, milud, kinsmen."

"These Adamses—are they, then, on opposite sides of the fence?" Lord Hemynge asked.

This was Tom's great chance to reaffirm his forced policy of mystery. No set of facts he must report had ever backed him as the present complexities did.

"Milud," he intoned, "if there be a fence, no man knows today who stands on which side of it. There's many a gate and stile through it, and many a man may pass it without mark. It ain't what you'd expect to see, Lord Hemynge—but there it be, milud, ready for your viewing tomorrow."

"Be damned to your oracles, Tom," the peer exploded. "You're certainly pushing me toward that bench. Well, you've been on the spot, and you know what I want. I submit to your impudence." He paused. "Have you got me a decent lodging, Tom?"

"Indeed, sir, a pretty mansion on the mall. Only, the offer is made from Mr. Hutchinson, the Lieutenant Governor, not my doing, sir. It will serve you handsome for such entertainment as you may wish to offer the *Sons o' Liberty*, milud."

Lord Hemynge was actually nettled by the monstrous impudence of Tom's last utterance—and especially by the fact

36

that the expression upon his face as he spoke it could not have been more sublimely innocent.

"Arrange me for bed," his lordship ordered. Tompkins obeyed with alacrity and deftness.

In a bleak hour before dawn Lord Hemynge was awakened gently by Tompkins. The faithful servant had stirred up a lively blaze at the hearth and had lighted candles, but the extreme cold that penetrated the chamber gave the peer a new insight into the rigors of the New England climate. Tompkins brought him some strange garments, which he had warmed before the fire, urging his master to put them on next to his skin. Lord Hemynge examined these heavy woolen undergarments, which were very long in the drawers, with an extreme distaste; and he might have summoned sufficient resistance to reject them except that they had been warmed. His lordship rather quarreled with Tompkins about them, but Tom's nagging was relentless.

The toilet complete, Tompkins guided his patron to the officers' mess, where Colonel Dalrymple stood drinking hot tea and rum from a great mug. The commander greeted his guest with a decent inexpressiveness, suited to the hour and the temperature, and offered him a similar brew. The party was completed by Captain Preston, a slender and handsome young officer, whose air of carrying an oppressive burden of injustice may have been due to the natural conditions of the hour, Lord Hemynge thought; and by Tompkins. All four stood as they drank the steaming liquid and ate fragments of broken dry bread set on a platter on the table. Lord Hemynge had never felt less affable, but as the brew warmed his vitals he began to feel a noticeable respect for, even a gratitude to, these companions who so sensibly maintained silence at such a moment.

The Colonel indicated presently that it was time to move on to the landing. The walk through stony courtyards, past an occasional sentinel who seemed frozen at his post, to the dreadful dampness of the small wharf was a punishment that he, at least, did not deserve, Lord Hemynge felt. Here the young captain took a morose leave of the party. (His person was unsafe in Boston without an armed guard as escort.)

It was a little better in the boat, for a canopy had been erected amidships, and a small brazier of hot coals was placed at the feet of the commander and the envoy. Even so, Lord Hemynge was grateful now to Tompkins for forcing him into the woolens that encased his limbs. Without them he must have suffered a damaging chill.

Reviewing in his thoughts the explanations of the Boston situation the Colonel had given him very briefly while they supped alone last night, Lord Hemynge recalled that young Captain Preston was the officer who had been in command of the troops on the fatal fifth of March, when the incident had occurred that had resulted in the eight soldiers being held on charges of murder. It was clear from the Colonel's remarks that he and his staff, marooned now by "request" of the civil magistrates of the Massachusetts Bay provincial government in the bleak fastness of Castle William, were concerned deeply by the predicament of those private soldiers. The brooding, aggrieved air of the junior officer, and the quiet, watchful anxiety that told in the manner of the Colonel were the only expressions they had allowed themselves of the natural resentment they must feel. While recognizing the kind of seasoning into grim resignation, in the face of civilian incompetencies and whims of conduct, that could be inculcated into old campaigners by the discipline of the armed forces, Lord Hemynge was amazed by the preoccupation of these military men with correct behavior.

When the Earl had suggested that the civil administration of the province had shown a considerable weakness, the Colonel had responded by expressing sympathy for Mr. Hutchinson: "He has done his best—done well, in the circumstances, sir." And the commander of the accused troops had pointedly not indulged in any intimation that this "best" or this "well" was far from being good enough.

38

When Lord Hemynge expressed surprise that General Gage, the general in command in America, had remained in New York throughout the difficulty, the Colonel refused to subscribe by the bat of an eyelid to an implied proposition that his own command was suffering neglect from the General. The newly arrived envoy from the ministry at this point formed a critical hostility to General Gage, and privately wished such a rapid series of promotions might be the Colonel's lot that he should swiftly replace Gage.

The Colonel was undoubtedly an intense partisan of his men in the current trial. But his scruples with respect to the constitutional supremacy of civil government and his awe in the face of due process of English law prevented his expressing his partisanship with the choler that would seem appropriate.

Seated in the skiff beside the heavy-bodied, anxious-eyed army officer, Lord Hemynge was conscious of a special liking for him. He admired the man's incapacity to complain; he admired his fidelity to duty; and he admired his forbearance. But most of all, he admired the quality of scrupulousness in this old campaigner, long accustomed to command, that led him to recognize the limits of his authority.

As they parted on the Customs wharf landing at the town shore, the Colonel detained the peer for a moment. "I am grateful that you are here to witness a portion of this trial, my lord," he said in a low tone. "I am confident that the fact you come direct from the ministry will make itself felt."

Lord Hemynge, far from certain how his presence in Boston might "make itself felt," bowed in acknowledgment.

The Colonel and an aide walked off into the misty shadows of Ship Street. Tompkins had secured a chaise, and bundled his frozen patron into it.

At a quarter before nine o'clock Lord Hemynge and his companion joined a crowd in Queen Street. From there they entered the Town House and found their way to seats in the courtroom. His lordship was pleased to observe that the large white chamber was decently ornamented with draperies of a heavy red stuff, and that the great seats awaiting the justices were upholstered in a handsome red plush. He was especially relieved to notice that the hall was heated by several fires, beside each of which stood an attendant with a basket of wood.

From the information given to him variously by Tompkins and Colonel Dalrymple, Lord Hemynge knew that the indictment presented to the four justices of His Majesty's Superior Court of Judicature, Court of Assize and General Gaol Delivery at Boston, submitted as a true bill by the jurors of the King, set forth that Thomas Preston, Esquire, Captain of a company of troops in the 29th Regiment of Foot, and eight men of his company, designated as the laborers Wemms, Hartegan, M'Cauley, White, Killroy, Warren, Carrol, and Montgomery, not having the fear of God before their eyes, but being moved and seduced by the instigation of the devil and their own wicked hearts, did, on the fifth day of this instant March, with force and arms, and of their malice aforethought, commit felony and murder, against the peace of the King, his crown and dignity. The result of their action, in which William Warren was named effectively most foul offender, but in which all did aid and abet this Warren, was the death of five men of Boston, unarmed, one Crispus Attucks being named as the immediate victim, having received two mortal wounds from bullets propelled by the explosion of gunpowder, one of said wounds having the extent of a depth of six inches and a width of one inch in the right breast a little below the right pap, the other mortal wound having the extent also of a depth of six inches and a width of one inch in the left breast of said Attucks, a little below the left pap.

The indictment also provided details concerning the deaths of Samuel Grey, Samuel Maverick, James Caldwell, and Patrick Carr. Lord Hemynge was informed that the Honorables Benjamin Lynde, John Cushing, Peter Oliver, and Edmund Trowbridge were the justices, and that among these the Honor-

40

able Peter Oliver was a brother-in-law to the Acting Governor of the Massachusetts Bay, His Honor, Thomas Hutchinson, Lieutenant Governor and former Chief Justice.

Both Colonel Dalrymple and Tompkins had dwelt upon the peculiar balance of forces represented in prosecution counsel for the Crown and defense counsel for the prisoners. Samuel Quincy, known as a reasonable, reliable King's man, had accepted the odd position of pressing the Crown's charge of murder against the troopers of His Majesty's forces. Aligned with him for the prosecution was Robert Treat Paine, a thoroughly respectable lawyer, regarded as free at least of damning commitment either to the "Patriot" or to the "Prerogative" party.

Engaged to lead in defense of the soldiers against the charges was one John Adams, kinsman to the Samuel who was known as the very father of the Sons of Liberty, and himself a close associate of such defiant and troubling "patriots" as James Otis, who had presented the arguments against the writs of assistance, nine years earlier—the first great Bostonian contention against rightful enactments of Parliament. In the recent sessions of the General Court at Cambridge, this Adams and his cousin had drafted the most defiant and insubordinate of the Legislature's replies to the messages and recommendations of the Acting Royal Governor, Mr. Hutchinson. Yet, Tompkins whispered to his lordship, John Adams' loyalty to the Crown had been in sufficient repute two years ago to merit an offer of appointment to serve as advocate general in the Court of Admiralty, tendered by the then Governor Bernard, surely on the prompting of Hutchinson. But Adams had refused the post. Now, against the popular outcries of his fellow townsmen of Boston, this man of a lone independent hand was defending the soldiers of the King who had "murdered" his compatriots! Lord Hemynge could appreciate Tompkins' insistence that confusion was being compounded in Boston.

The breaks in the fence were further opened by the alignment with Adams, for the defense, of Josiah Quincy, Junior, a man

41

very young in the profession of law, and a brother of the Samuel Quincy who headed the prosecution.

"It doth truly appear there must be some quarrels among the Boston cousinhoods come out of this, milud!" was Tompkins' sage conclusion.

"Let us pray they get up no more bloody massacres over it," was the peer's dry note.

Lord Hemynge had begun to notice that the heat from the royal fires in the courtroom was creating an undesirable mortification of his flesh, wrapped as it was in the enormous woolen undergarments Tompkins had forced him into, when the processional entrance of the four justices occurred. The close-packed assemblage rose, to stand until the personages in wigs and scarlet robes had seated themselves. It was momentarily quite like the Old Bailey, Lord Hemynge pleasantly thought.

Justice Trowbridge ordered the prisoners to be brought in, and the entry of the eight private soldiers was observed in a general hush. Perhaps because he knew they had lately been in garrison at Dublin, Lord Hemynge observed an unmistakable Irish quality in several of the faces. They all had an air of trouble about them—at least, of being caught in an unholy scrape; and even in their bright uniforms they had somehow a ragged appearance.

Now Colonel Dalrymple, brilliant in his scarlet coat, rose from a seat in the front of the hall and stepped quickly to the rail of the dock. He spoke to the first prisoner, so low that the fellow had to lean over and put his hand to his ear. The "laborer"—it was Matthew Killroy—began to nod and smile, and the officer quickly stepped back to his seat as a bailiff moved toward him to restore order.

Lord Hemynge glanced questioningly at Tompkins, who looked back at his patron with an air of consideration, then shifted closer to the peer, indicating that he might vouchsafe a comment. Leaning sideward to submit his ear to his secretary's rasping whisper, Lord Hemynge appeared to be condescending.

"The Colonel do have a word for his men in the dock every day, milud," was Tompkins' news.

"Oh?" murmured the Earl, suffering from a shudder induced by Tom's breath in his ear. Then he felt the need to review a point the Colonel had passed over briefly. "The Captain— Preston?—is not held with the other prisoners? His trial is over —he is free?"

Again the thin chapped lips and the breath at his ear. "Yes, milud, his trial was over by the end of October, under the same indictment. They could produce no proof that 'twas he give the order to fire, night of March the fifth."

"Oh, yes," said his lordship. "Did he have the same counsel for defense?"

Tompkins nodded affirmatively, but demanded another attendance of the ear. "Johnny Adams, milud!" He drew back quickly, watching his patron as though to detect whether he appreciated properly the significance of counsel's identity.

Lord Hemynge could stand no more of the torment of receiving Tom's whispers, and looked again toward the prisoners. He noticed that the word of the Colonel had been passed along from man to man, and that the fellows appeared to have been considerably cheered by the communication, whatever it was. One or two of them leaned forward to catch the officer's eye, and when they succeeded they smiled and nodded, and made minor saluting gestures. (The news that the Colonel had divulged to Killroy was that a commissioner had only just arrived from the ministry in London to observe the trial—no less than a peer, vested surely with special powers from the Lord Chancellor or the Lord Chief Justice Mansfield to assure that justice be done in the Massachusetts Bay—to these prisoners, of course.)

Then Justice Trowbridge brought the court to order, and called Mr. Josiah Quincy, Junior, to resume for the prisoners at the bar.

There was something fragile, innocent, and hopeful in the

43

appearance of this slender young advocate (which included a slight crossing of the eyes) that made an immediate appeal to the sympathetic strain in Lord Hemynge's humors. Yet the firmness and fluency with which he began to speak quickly modified the tale told by his physical aspect and youth.

"Let us take a transient view of some occurrences preceding and subsequent to the melancholy fifth of March," the young man began. "About some five or six years ago, it is well known, certain measures were adopted by the British Parliament which gave a general alarm to this continent. A sentiment universally prevailed that our dearest rights were invaded. I need not inform you how the tide rose as we were advancing toward the present times. A vast majority thought all that was dear was at stake—sentiments of liberty—property—ignominious bondage —all conspired to increase the ferment.

"At this period the troops land.

"Let us here pause, and view the citizen and the soldier.

"The causes of grievance being thus spread far and wide, the inhabitants viewed the soldiery as called in to force obedience to acts which were, in general, deemed subversive of natural as well as constitutional freedom.

"I say, gentlemen, and appeal to you for the truth of what I say, that many on this continent viewed their chains as already forged, they saw fetters as prepared, they beheld the soldiers as fastening, and riveting for ages, the shackles of their bondage. With the justness of these apprehensions, you and I have nothing to do in this place. Disquisitions of this sort are for the Senate and the chamber of council—they are for statesmen and politicians, who take a latitude in thoughts and actions."

Lord Hemynge at this point raised a kerchief to his lips with a seemly gesture.

"But we, gentlemen, are confined in our excursions by the rigid rules of law. You are to think, judge, and act as jurymen, and not as statesmen."

("Statesmen and politicians, who take a latitude . . ." Yes,

44

Lord Hemynge was enjoying himself. "You are . . . jurymen . . . not . . . statesmen." Indeed, he was enjoying himself.)

"Matters being thus circumstanced, what might be expected?

"No room was left for cordiality and friendship. Discontent was seated on almost every brow. Instead of that hospitality that the soldier thought himself entitled to, scorn, contempt, and silent murmurs were his reception. Almost every countenance lowered with a discontented gloom, and scarce an eye but flashed indignant fire.

"Turn and contemplate the camp. Do we find a more favorable appearance? The soldier had his feelings, his sentiments, and his characteristic passions also. The constitution of our government has provided a stimulus for his affections—the pride of conscious virtue, the sense of valor, the point of honor. The law had taught him to think favorably of himself, had taught him to consider himself as peculiarly appointed for the safeguard and defence of his country. He had heard that he put not off the citizen when he entered the camp; but because he was a citizen, and wished to continue so, he made himself for a while a soldier.

"How stinging was it to be stigmatized as the instrument of tyranny and oppression! How exasperating, to be viewed as aiding to enthrall his country! He felt his heart glow with an ardor which he took for a love of liberty and his country, and had formed to himself no design fatal to its privileges.

"The right of quartering troops in this province must be discussed at a different tribunal. They were sent here by that authority which our laws know; they were quartered here, as I take it, agreeable to an act of the British Parliament; they were ordered here by your Sovereign and mine.

"Had anyone told you some weeks ago that the evidence on the Crown side would have appeared in its present light, would you have believed it? Can anyone think it his duty to espouse the part acted by those assembled in King street? The inhabitants of Boston, by *no* rules of law, justice, or common sense, can be supposed answerable for the unjustifiable conduct of a few

45

individuals hastily assembled in the streets. You are, therefore, by no means to blend two things so essentially different as the guilt or innocence of this town and the prisoners together.

"Lest my opinion should not have any weight, let me remind you of an author whom I trust you will credit. You will not suspect him of being unfriendly to liberty. I am sure you ought to love and revere him. I allude to the third letter of the Farmer of Pennsylvania to his Countrymen. 'The cause of liberty,' says that great and good writer, 'is a cause of too much dignity to be sullied by turbulence and tumult. Those who engage in it should breathe a sedate yet fervent spirit animating them to actions of prudence, justice, modesty, bravery, humanity, and magnanimity.'

"What has transpired on this trial savoring of any of these virtues? Was it justice or humanity to attack, insult, ridicule, and abuse a single sentinel on his post? Was it either modest, brave, or magnanimous to rush upon the points of fixed bayonets, and trifle, vapor, and provoke at the very mouths of loaded muskets? It may be brutal rage or wanton rashness, but not surely any true magnanimity.

"To finish with the justly celebrated Farmer. 'Hot, rash, disorderly proceedings injure the reputation of a people as to wisdom, valor and virtue without procuring the least benefit.'

"We ought to recollect that our present decisions will be scanned perhaps through all Europe. We must not forget that we ourselves will have a reflective hour—when the pulse will no longer beat with the tumults of the day—when the conscious pang of having betrayed truth, justice, and integrity shall bite like a serpent.

"Consider, gentlemen, the danger which you, and all of us are in, of being led away by our affections and attachments. We have seen the blood of our fellow men flowing in the streets. We have been told that this blood was wrongfully shed. This is now the point in issue. But let it be borne deep upon our minds that the prisoners are to be condemned by the evidence here in court produced against them, and by nothing else. We have gone at length through the evidence in behalf of the prisoners."

Here Tompkins secured once more his lordship's ear: "Two tedious days of it, milud—I sat through it all."

"In consideration of the law pertinent upon this evidence," Mr. Quincy, Junior, went on, "the law indulges no man in being his own avenger. Early in the history of jurisprudence we find the sword taken from the party injured and put into the hands of the magistrate. It saps the very root of distributive justice when any individual invades the prerogative of law, and snatches from the civil magistrate the balance and the rod. Let me inform you that the law which is to pass upon these prisoners is a law adapting itself to the human species with all their feelings, passions, and infirmities; a law which does not go upon the absurd supposition that men are stocks and stones, or that in fervor of the blood a man can act with the deliberation and judgment of a philosopher. No, gentlemen: the law supposes that a principle of resentment, for wise and obvious reasons, is deeply implanted in the human heart, and not to be eradicated by the efforts of state policy. It therefore in some degree conforms itself to all the workings of the passions, to which it pays a great indulgence—so far as not to be wholly incompatible with the wisdom, the good order, and the very being of government.

" 'You lobster!'—'You bloody-back!'—'You coward!'—'You dastard!'—are but some of the expressions proved. What words more galling? What more cutting and provoking to a soldier? —'You coward!' A soldier and a coward? This was touching— with a witness—the point of honor and the pride of virtue. But does the soldier step out of his ranks to seek his revenge? Not a witness pretends it. Does the law allow one member of the community to behave in this manner towards his fellow citizen, and then bid the injured party be calm and moderate? Does common sense, does the law, expect impossibilities? Here, to expect equanimity of temper would be as irrational as to expect discretion in a mad man!"

In his close, Mr. Quincy, Junior, made a clear demonstration that the assembly of the soldiers in the night of March the fifth was entirely lawful, whereas that of the citizens tormenting them surely was not lawful. Lord Hemynge found himself able to concur in this point, and also in the lines with which Mr. Quincy closed his pleading:

"The quality of mercy is not strain'd;
It droppeth as the gentle rain from heaven. . . .
it is twice blest;
It blesseth him that gives and him that takes."

48

4

Now there was an interval before counsel for the prisoners would proceed. Lord Hemynge leisurely looked about the courtroom, letting his gaze rest here on groups, there upon an individual person. From Mr. Quincy's hour he had gained a sense of initiation into some of the mysteries of Boston. On coming to witness these proceedings at the bar of English justice, he had conceived that in this assemblage of observers he was sitting among the populace of a rebellious, insubordinate, defiant, colonial seaport town. Mr. Quincy's assurance that the guilt or innocence of the townsfolk of Boston was not at stake in the trial, that the opponents of the soldiers in the incident of March the fifth had engaged only a small, unrepresentative group of citizens unlawfully assembled, had somehow given a face of respectability to the Boston folk gathered here to view the proceedings in the Superior Court. Gazing on them with this degree of enlightenment in his mind, Lord Hemynge could not help being struck by the difference between the present assemblage and one he might have seen at the Old Bailey in London. He was certain that many of those present were "people of the town"—artisans, laborers, small tradesmen—but he saw nowhere the slightly ratlike sharpness of countenance that was almost universal among such folk in the great capital of the British Empire.

Scattered through the throng were some who from the superior quality of their dress must be accounted gentry or thereabouts. However, these same persons were singularly free of fopperies of fashion, and it occurred to the Earl that this would not have been the case in London. There, the minor gentry were more affected by the example of persons of fashion than they quite recognized.

As the peer's gaze traveled, one man caught his eye, and one woman. The man had risen from his seat toward the front of the hall, and had moved to speak to several gentlemen sitting near by. He was tall, thin, of a gravely handsome countenance; his hair was decently powdered, and his black broadcloth coat was perfectly tailored.

"That be Mr. Hutchinson, Acting Governor of the province," Tompkins reported.

The woman he noticed was seated in a raised rank between two others who were in conversation across her. A grey gown, a blue shawl, and a blue and grey bonnet set off her brown hair and animated dark eyes to advantage. When she turned to speak to one of the women beside her, it was apparently with humor and spirit.

Again Tompkins did not miss the direction of his patron's gaze. "That be Mrs. Adams, wife to the barrister who takes up now, milud."

John Adams, Esquire, chief counsel for the defense, rose and moved to a position within the enclosure from which he could face the justices or the jury, at will. Lord Hemynge judged that he was in the more advanced middle years of life. (Tompkins later amended this impression: "Thirty-five years be his age, milud.") Somewhat short of stature, he gave the impression of having made a good start toward corpulence. His robe was black, and his tie wig had the appearance of being somehow a more modest one than those of the counsel opposing him. The figure and visage were not commanding on the merits of appearance alone. But there was a sense of anticipation in the

50

crowded hall that affected Lord Hemynge, too, and created a mood receptive to what this man might say or do.

The Earl had a breathing space in which he attempted to restore a decent skepticism to his own faculties of attention and judgment, when the man began to speak in a tone carrying a strong directness of vigor, and an aggressiveness of assertion, that provided striking contrast to the almost melodious persuasiveness of the junior counsel.

"May it please your honors, and you, gentlemen of the jury: I am for the prisoners at the bar and shall apologize for it only in the words of the Marquis Beccaria: 'If I can but be the instrument of preserving one life, his blessing and tears of transport shall be a sufficient consolation to me for the contempt of mankind.' "

That decent skepticism with which Lord Hemynge had sought to arm his faculties began a retreat, and presently, as a force, was dispelled. The tone and manner, the passionate sincerity of the speaker would brook no resistance. They did not invite, they commanded attention.

"We find in the rules laid down by the greatest English judges, who have been the brightest of mankind, we are to look upon it as more beneficial that many guilty persons should escape unpunished, than one innocent person should suffer. The reason is . . . it is of more importance to the community that innocence should be protected than it is that guilt should be punished; for guilt and crimes are so frequent in the world, that all of them cannot be punished; and many times they happen in such a manner that it is not of much consequence to the public whether they are punished or not. But when innocence itself is brought to the bar and condemned, especially to die, the subject will exclaim, 'It is immaterial to me whether I behave well or ill, for virtue itself is no security.' And if such a sentiment as this should take place in the mind of the subject, there would be an end to all security whatsoever."

On hearing these expressions, Lord Hemynge understood

why the attendance of his own skepticism was unnecessary. The mind of the speaker was so well furnished with a decent skepticism that it gained the confidence of all those among his hearers who were capable of doubt.

"I will read the words of the law itself. The rules I shall produce to you from Chief Justice Hale, whose character as a lawyer, a man of learning and philosophy, and as a Christian, will be disputed by nobody living; one of the greatest and best characters the English nation ever produced. His words are these: 'Tutius semper est errare in acquietando quam in puniendo; ex parte misericordiae quam ex parte justitiae.' It is always safer to err in acquitting than in punishing; on the part of mercy than the part of justice.

"From the same authority: 'Tutius erratur ex parte mitiori.' It is always safer to err on the milder side. The best rule in doubtful cases is rather to incline to acquittal than conviction. 'Quod dubitas, ne feceris.' Where you are doubtful, never act; that is, if you doubt of the prisoner's guilt, never declare him guilty. This is always the rule, especially in cases of life. Another rule from the same author: It is better five guilty persons should escape unpunished than one innocent person should die.

"The next authority shall be from another judge, of equal character, considering the age in which he lived—that is, Chancellor Fortesque, in praise of the laws of England. This is a very ancient writer on the English law. His words are: 'Indeed one would rather, much rather, that twenty guilty persons escape the punishment of death than one innocent person be condemned, and suffer capitally.'

"Lord Chief Justice Hale says it is better five guilty persons escape than one innocent person suffer. Lord Chancellor Fortesque, you see, carries the matter farther, and says, indeed one had rather, much rather, that twenty guilty persons should escape, than one innocent person suffer capitally.

"Indeed, this rule is not peculiar to the English law. There never was a system of laws in the world in which this rule did not prevail. It prevailed in the ancient Roman law, and, which is more remarkable, it prevails in the modern Roman law; even the judges in the Courts of Inquisition, who with racks, burnings, and scourges examine criminals, even there they preserve it as a maxim that it is better the guilty should escape punishment than the innocent suffer—'Satis esse nocentem absolvi quam insontem damnari!'

"This is the temper we ought to set out with, and these the rules we are to be governed by. And I shall take it for granted as a first principle that the eight prisoners at the bar had better all be acquitted, though we should admit them all to be guilty, than that any one of them should by your verdict be found guilty, being innocent.

"The action now before you is homicide; that is, the killing of one man by another. The law calls it homicide, but it is not criminal in all cases for one man to slay another. Had the prisoners been on the Plains of Abraham and slain an hundred Frenchmen apiece, the English law would have considered it as a commendable action, virtuous and praiseworthy."

The reference to the Plains of Abraham moved Lord Hemynge to a silent but exultant cry of "Hear, hear!" The memory of Massachusetts Bay was by those words driven back to the days of high partnership between the Old England and the New—to the tragic victory at Quebec, achieved by the courage and blood of regular troops and colonial militia, under the inspired government of the Great Commoner, William Pitt. When had an Empire moved more nobly than Great Britain to deliver her remote children, her loyal colonies, from the oppressive hazard of being neighbor to an ancient autocracy, a crusted and ignoble tyranny! The sound of the name of the Plains of Abraham must call to the mind of every true-born Englishman—and these of Massachusetts Bay were still true-born, Lord Hemynge would take his oath on it—not only the greatness of Pitt, but the greatness of all things British. Thank ye, O learned judge—a Daniel come to judgment!

It seemed to Lord Hemynge that this courtroom in which he sat had become enlarged, that there was spaciousness in it now for the spirit of high responsibility, for awareness of great meanings. If only the speaker could connect these essences, this sense, this spirit, with the cause in hand . . . "Only connect them," he murmured to himself.

"But the fact," the advocate went on, "the fact was the slaying of five unhappy persons on that night. You are to consider whether it was justifiable, excuseable, or felonious; and if felonious, whether it was murder or manslaughter."

The Earl conceded in his mind that the man could make the connection. The constant movement he demanded from the general to the particular, from the high to the low, from the noble concept to the brutal condition was violent. He illumined the cause with a light that was not serene, but was brilliant and vibrating.

"The law has planted fences and barriers around every individual; it is a castle around every man's person, as well as his house. As the love of God and our neighbor comprehends the whole duty of man, so self-love and social comprehend all the duties we owe to mankind. The first branch is self-love, which is not only our indisputable right, but our clearest duty. By the laws of nature this is interwoven in the heart of every individual. God almighty, whose laws we cannot alter, has implanted it there, and we can annihilate ourselves as easily as root out this affection for ourselves. It is the first and strongest principle in our nature. Justice Blackstone calls it 'the primary canon in the law of nature.' The rules of the common law which authorize a man to preserve his own life at the expense of another's are not contradicted by any divine or moral law. We talk of liberty and property, but, if we cut up the law of self-defence, we cut up the foundation of both—and if we give this up, the rest is of very little value.

"You must place yourselves in the situation of Wemms or Killroy."

Lord Hemynge reflected that the speaker had brought him to a condition in which he was willing to do even this.

"Consider yourselves as knowing that the prejudices of the world about you were against you; that the people about you thought you came to dragoon them into obedience to statutes, instructions, mandates, and edicts which they thoroughly detested; that they, the soldiers, had no friends about them; the people shouting, huzzaing, and 'making the mob whistle,' as they call it,—which, when a boy makes it in the street is no formidable thing, but when made by a multitude is a most hideous shriek, almost as terrible as an Indian yell; the people crying 'kill them! kill them! knock them over!'—heaving snowballs, oyster shells, clubs, white birch sticks three inches and a half in diameter—consider yourselves in this situation and then judge whether a reasonable man in the soldier's situation would not have concluded that they were going to kill him."

Then the speaker made a transition that for no evident reason caused that familiar tingle to spread over the envoy's nerves.

"There is no occasion for the magistrate to read the riot act."

That was all there was to it—yet it somehow had the effect of a formidable flash of wit. It dashed the hearer from the scene of violence and fury in Brattle Square, months past in remoteness, to the dry order of the courtroom.

"In the case before you, I suppose you will be satisfied, when you come to examine the witnesses and compare the evidence with rules of the common law, abstracted from all mutiny acts and articles of war, that these soldiers were in such a situation that they could not help themselves. People were coming from Royal Exchange lane and other parts of the town with clubs and cord-wood sticks. The soldiers were planted by the Custom House. They could not retreat. They were surrounded on all sides, for there were people behind them as well as before them. All the party concerned in this unlawful design were guilty of what any one of them did. If any body threw a snowball, it was the act of the whole party. If any struck with a club, or threw a club, and the club had killed any body, the whole party would have been guilty of murder in law.

55

"This is the policy of the law: to discourage and prevent riots, insurrections, turbulence, and tumults. In the continual vicissitudes of human things, amidst the shocks of fortune and the whirls of passion that take place at certain critical seasons even in the mildest government, the people are liable to run into riots and tumults. There are churchquakes and statequakes in the moral and political world as well as earthquakes, storms and tempests in the physical."

The *"churchquakes and statequakes"* settled one thing: Lord Hemynge now knew the object of his mission. It was to secure this man for the House of Lords—to make him a colleague with Chatham, Mansfield, and the others in the government of the British Empire by King, Lords, and Commons; to secure for him a platform from which his voice might become known to Burke, Rockingham, Barré, and the rest—yes, even to Wilkes. The emissary of His Majesty's Government settled back in his seat now, certain that whatever else might be unfolded by the swooping energy of this John Novanglus, the die was cast. All the arts of negotiation and seduction, if necessary, must be engaged to secure this one new voice, this new element of power and integrity, vigor, freshness, and cleanness, for the House of Lords. The doubts expressed in the humid bed-chamber at Hayes by the Great Commoner himself must be proved baseless. And now it was as though John Adams had caught some emanation of his lordship's thought, for immediately he spoke forth on a philosophy of government—unlike his Quincy colleague, quite unabashed to reveal a vein of high statesmanship in his mind:

"It is a general, if not an universal truth that the aptitude of the people to mutinies, seditions, tumults and insurrections is in direct proportion to the despotism of the government. In governments completely despotic, where the will of one man is the only law, this disposition is most prevalent; in aristocracies next; in mixed monarchies, less than either of the former; in complete republics, least of all. Under the same form of

56

government, as in a limited monarchy, for example, the virtue and wisdom of the administration may generally be measured by the peace and order that are seen among the people.

"However this may be, such is the imperfection of all things in the world, that no form of government, and perhaps no wisdom or virtue in the administration, can at all times avoid riots and disorders among the people."

Lord Hemynge recognized that the statement of these views implied a capacity in the people, or at least in lawyers, to judge the "virtue and wisdom" of an administration. He knew that the King, and his chief ministers in London, would regard the affirmation that such a capacity existed and should be exercised, as—at the very least—insolent. The visiting peer himself had doubts as to the safety of a state in which such views had wide currency—but on this shore, remote from the council chambers of Westminster, he found he had an unexpected tolerance for the fresh and vigorous expression of them.

The barrister now was on "provocation." The citations he submitted made it clear that assault, in the eyes of the law, is so intolerable a provocation that the intended victim of the assault may kill in self-defense, and the killing be defined as manslaughter, not murder. He conceded one point, however:

"Insolent, scurrilous, or slanderous language, when it precedes an assault, aggravates it. But words of reproach, how grating and offensive soever, are in the eye of the law, no provocation in the case of voluntary homicide."

Mr. Adams then undertook a review of the testimony of witnesses, seeking to prove that the provocation offered to the soldiers was the threat and the reality of physical assault, accompanied in words by the aggravating scurrility. Take the evidence of one Ebenezer Bridgham:

"This is a witness for the Crown, and his testimony is of great weight for the prisoners. He swears positively that he not only saw ice or snow thrown, but the guns struck several times. He swears positively there were a dozen of persons with clubs surrounded the soldiers' party. Twelve sailors with clubs were by much an overmatch to eight soldiers, chained there by the order and command of their officer, to stand in defence of their sentry; not only so, but under an oath to stand there—that is, to obey the lawful command of their officer—as much, gentlemen of the jury, as you are under oath to determine this cause by law and evidence. It was in the power of the sailors to kill one half or the whole of the party if they had been so disposed. What had the soldiers to expect when twelve persons armed with clubs—*sailors,* too, between whom and *soldiers* there is such an antipathy that they fight as naturally when they meet as the elephant and the rhinoceros—were daring enough even at the time they were loading their guns, to come up with their clubs and smite on the guns? What had eight soldiers to expect from such a set of people? Would it have been a prudent resolution in them, or in any body in their situation, to have stood still to see if the sailors would knock their brains out or not?

"We have been entertained with a great variety of phrases to avoid calling this sort of people tormenting the soldiers, a *mob.* Some call them shavers, some call them geniuses. Why we should scruple to call such a set of people a mob, I can't conceive, unless the name is too respectable for them. The sun is not about to stand still or go out, nor the rivers to dry up, because there was a mob in Boston, on the fifth of March, that attacked a party of soldiers. Such things are not new in the world, nor in the British dominions, though they are comparative rarities and novelties in this town."

Lord Hemynge found himself surrendered very completely to the appeals of the extravagant and the grotesque in the speaker's progress. He was also beginning to make an inspired guess about the peculiar sensibilities of "this town." The logic was unassailable: imperfections and evils that were old in the world could properly be declared "novelties" in Boston because of the brief existence of this high-minded seaport in history. Yet his lordship could not help suspecting that this logic would

ever be applied, locally, to virtues and graces that were old in
he world.

"From the nature of things," John Adams asserted, "soldiers
uartered in a populous town will always occasion two mobs,
'here they prevent one. *They are wretched conservators of
he peace.*"

This statement unaccountably stirred in the Earl of Hemynge
powerful impulse to cheer. Yet no one of the spectators in
he courtroom, not even Tompkins, would have suspected from
is appearance that the visitor from London was so moved.

What struck him so forcibly was that John Adams made his
ssertion as though it were a bald declaration of the obvious.
erhaps it was. Perhaps everyone knew that what the lawyer
ad stated was a fact. But throughout history, kings, tyrants,
ziers, consuls, governments, ministries, had ruled unanimously
s though the opposite were true—as though, when peace in
opulous towns were threatened, soldiers were the only extant
onservators" who might be called upon to preserve it. The
ew England lawyer's refutation of this received tradition was
t forth with some bitterness, but also with an assurance that
dicated he was confident his hearers were certain to be in
greement with him at least on this point. Here, indeed, was
atter for long consideration in the Senate and the Council
hamber, for statesmen and politicians to review soberly before
king their latitudes.

As the speaker moved on again to further examination of
idence and testimony submitted to the Court by witnesses of
e events of March the fifth, Lord Hemynge gave in to the
tigue induced by close attention, and ceased to follow the
gument. He had heard enough to recognize that John Adams
ossessed the power of eloquence and was master of it. He was
nvinced that he had found a colonial lawyer who might be
atched in debate with any orator in Lords or Commons—
ve only Chatham. And the Massachusetts Bay genius had in
mmon with the Pitt genius the capacity to use surprise as a
eans to an end. Chatham's surprises were calculated with the

craft of a theatrical wizard. Adams, on the other hand, sub
mitted his surprises as though they were mere common sense
with an effect that was both rude and welcome. It was as thoug
Chatham had drunk from the deeply walled and guarded well
of ancient wisdom and artfulness, and Adams had drunk from
some wild bubbling fountain of truth, springing uncontaine
in the deep forest. There was a touch of the Pharaoh abou
Chatham, whose law sometimes was his own penetratin
vision—"*I* rejoice that America has resisted!" And Adams, wit
his veneration of Law, was closer akin to the Mosaic—a kinshi
altogether lacking in the Lord Chief Justice Mansfield, wit
the dry authority of his immense learning, his penny-pinchin
exactitude, his contemptuous watchful waiting for Chathai
to blunder. No—here in the New England was a voice sound
ing forth in fresh, untainted notes of a daylight music—simpl
modern, and daring.

The Earl of Hemynge was proud of his discovery.

Mr. Adams came at last to his peroration, and said so clearly
"I will enlarge no more on the evidence, but submit it to yo

"Facts are stubborn things. And whatsoever may be ou
wishes, our inclinations, or the dictates of our passions, the
cannot alter the state of facts and evidence. Nor is the law le
stable than the fact.

"To your candor and justice I submit the prisoners and the
cause. The law in all vicissitudes of government, fluctuatio
of the passions, or flights of enthusiasm will preserve a stead
undeviating course. It will not bend to the uncertain wishe
imaginations, and wanton tempers of men.

"To use the words of a great and worthy man, a patriot an
an hero, an enlightened friend of mankind, and a martyr t
liberty—I mean Algernon Sidney. 'The law,' says he, 'no passio
can disturb. 'Tis devoid of desire and fear, lust and anger. 'T
"mens sine affectu"—written reason—retaining some measui
of the divine perfection. It does not enjoin that which please
a weak, frail man, but without regard to persons, command

60

hat which is good and punishes evil in all, whether rich or poor,
igh or low. 'Tis deaf, inexorable, inflexible. On the one hand it
s inexorable to the cries and lamentations of the prisoner; on
he other, it is deaf, deaf as an adder, to the clamors of the
opulace.'"

Then it was over.

Lord Hemynge and Tompkins rose, as did many others. The
Earl had a glimpse of Mr. Josiah Quincy, Junior, moving swiftly
cross the enclosure to grasp the hand of his colleague. Then,
y strenuous effort, order was restored for a brief moment,
giving Justice Trowbridge an opportunity to adjourn the court
ill the trial should be resumed the next day.

Again the crowd was in motion, almost in agitation, with all
moving toward the doors.

"Come, Tom," Lord Hemynge murmured, "get me to the
odging that has been set aside for us as quickly as possible.
must remove these hair shirts you have forced on my limbs."

"I may remind your ludship that His Honor, Lieutenant
Governor Hutchinson, is to meet your ludship there. If he be
wift, sir, it may be your grace will wish to receive his ad-
resses—within the woolens?" Tom queried innocently.

"Not of my own choice," said the Earl firmly. "I think you
aid there was a major-domo sort of servant attached to the
quarters—was his name Moses?"

"No, milud. 'Tis Aaron he be called. A servingman much
avored by Sir Francis Bernard, according to all reports."

They forced their way on out to the street, where the pale
watery sunshine did nothing to warm the Boston air. Tompkins
ummoned a carriage that had been put at Lord Hemynge's
isposal by the Acting Governor.

5

AFTER A SHORT DRIVE INTO WHAT TOMPKINS ANNOUNCED proudly was Marlborough Street, the carriage was stopped before a house of three stories, constructed of brick and surmounted by a neat white cupola. The peer followed his guide across a small garden space, in which several trees were well placed to afford summer shade. They mounted a flight of red freestone steps to a spacious porch, over which a balcony extended from the second floor. A wide double-leaved door was opened to Tompkins' ring by a Negro servant in a black livery.

"Lord Hemynge, to wait upon his honor, the Lieutenant Governor," Tom pronounced, rather puffily.

The servant bowed to pass them in, closed the door behind them. "His honor, the Lieutenant Governor, is awaiting the gentlemen, sir," he said.

Lord Hemynge studied the hall in which he stood momentarily, while the servant went to announce him. He recognized that elements of a late Tudor style had been adapted here with modesty and taste. Polished panels, turkey carpet, and other notes suggested that an impression of grandeur was intended. But there was something compressed and saved about the present mansion—the narrowness of the staircase, for example —that would not have been observed in a London house. Yet these notes of economy produced a lightness and clearness that were distinct merits. The same grace was more comfortably expanded in the spacious apartment into which Lord Hemynge followed the servant after hearing his name announced.

Mr. Hutchinson, elegant and dignified, was an even handsomer figure when met in close quarters than he had appeared when seen from a distance. As he advanced in greeting, Lord Hemynge noted that his linen was of that fine cloth most often imported from Holland.

"My lord," said Thomas Hutchinson, "I had been advised that we should have the pleasure of a visit from you by Lord Hillsborough, who holds you in high estimation."

"The same gentleman has commended your well known courtesies, sir," said Lord Hemynge, "and I have heard Sir Francis Bernard speak of you with the warmest regard."

The Acting Governor bowed. "He is all kindness, and is a man whose abilities are sadly missed here today. You visit us, my lord, in a time of tribulation."

"Yes—I have been made acquainted with the circumstances, at home and in the courtroom today. But I observe, sir, that you have powerful friends at court."

"You mean the counsel for the prisoners at the bar? Yes, it is true that Adams and Quincy present the case for the soldiers with effect. But I am afraid of the jury, my lord; the verdict is most uncertain."

"It may be of comfort to us, sir, to recall that though the law may be deaf—'deaf as an adder'—the jury is not."

The Earl noticed that Mr. Hutchinson was not altogether pleased to have the phrase used by the lawyer for the defense so quoted to him. A mood of perversity moved the envoy to press his insistence further with another reference: "I am confident, your honor, that the verdict, when it is given, will not add to the present 'statequakes and churchquakes' agitating Boston and London."

Mr. Hutchinson stared at Lord Hemynge briefly and decided to ignore the provocation. "We are grateful to hear that London is concerned, even as we are, my lord," he replied with dignity.

The Earl sobered. "I myself am here, sir, only because the government is gravely concerned."

Mr. Hutchinson bowed. "We must assume that your mission among us is one of high import, my lord. But my own purpose today is only to make you welcome in the province. This house is at your disposal as long as you will remain with us." The Lieutenant Governor went on to inform his guest that servants had been provided, and that his lordship's man, Tompkins, had been placed in command.

"You are most gracious, your excellency," said the peer. "I had no need, nor any wish, for so handsome a lodging."

"Your journey has been arduous. We are grateful that you have so swiftly shown your interest in our troubled concerns by visiting the court today, in spite of the fatigue of the long session. We must grant you time for refreshment and retirement."

Lord Hemynge was reminded of the flaming woolens that encircled his legs. Nobly he curbed his impatience to be rid of them. "I am confident that Lord Hillsborough himself, had he been here, must have been drawn to visit the court to witness this most astonishing trial."

"And he, too, my lord," said the proud Mr. Hutchinson, "must have been allowed an hour for retirement. May I expect the honor of your presence to dine at my seat at Milton tomorrow? I consider it not fit that I, a former chief justice of the province, should be present when the verdict is brought in. I have made arrangements to have news of it brought swiftly to me there."

Lord Hemynge saw the point. It might be considered likewise unsuitable that an emissary from the King's ministers in London should be present when the verdict was delivered. He accepted the invitation, and Mr. Hutchinson made his departure.

Then Tompkins was at hand.

"Come—help me remove these vile garments, Tom."

"Yes, milud."

"Ah—you might tell Moses that I shall be ready to sup in a quarter of an hour."

"Yes, milud. Only it be his brother, Aaron."

The Honorable Thomas Hutchinson, Esquire, Acting Governor of the Massachusetts Bay and Master of Milton Hill, was a gracious host. Lord Hemynge visited him alone, having left Tompkins to attend the final session of the trial.

The situation of the Hutchinson house at Milton was singularly pleasing even in the cold sunlight that exposed a wintry reduction in the charms of the surrounding landscape. A long avenue bounded by buttonwood trees (Lord Hemynge thought of them as plane trees) formed the approach to the height upon which the house and garden were placed. Mr. Hutchinson met his visitor at the portico as he stepped from his coach. Before inviting him to enter, the Governor pointed out the features of the view that had attracted him to the site, and that had not lost their capacity to please him through many years of familiarity.

An abundance of gently rounded blue hills extended from a more rugged west toward the sea in the east. A river, curiously named Neponset, flowed imperceptibly to the coast, in its later course making a turn to the north toward the town of Boston. "We sometimes speed guests bound for England downstream to a pike," Mr. Hutchinson said, "where they may take coach for the Dorchester Heights and board their ships at anchor offshore."

The chilled landscape had the aspect of a great park, quiescent, whose pastoral heart must be in its variety of groves—some of them leafless, some being evergreen groves of dark pine.

"I am sorry that you could not have been here two months ago, my lord, when our maples were in colour. There is in the mid-days of October a great glow of warmth from the sun, but

65

morning and evening are frosty. This makes for us a season of 'Indian summer' that is perhaps our best season. But it is all good," the Governor added rather to himself, "it is all good here in the Massachusetts."

Lord Hemynge was touched with admiration, both of the prospect and of the man. "The parks at Hayes and Stowe have no greater merits than this," he said quietly.

Mr. Hutchinson was not in the least surprised. "No—I suppose their splendid artificers cannot provide the natural advantages we enjoy in this country." He was so gravely considerate that Lord Hemynge felt rather put out. But he made no rejoinder, as his host was now leading him into the house.

This country manor-house enclosed space enough and comfort enough to be the family seat of any gentleman of birth and consequence. After he had toured the place guided by its master, whose manner was a pleasing mixture of pride, dignity and reserve, Lord Hemynge was willing to grant that it *was* the family seat of such a gentleman.

As the Governor and his guest dined, no others being present, Mr. Hutchinson spoke freely of the past. He told the peer many stories of New England, beginning with the history of his noble ancestress, Mistress Anne Hutchinson, the "Nonsuch," who emigrated from the Bay Colony to Rhode Island and late to Connecticut, driven by her conscience and her energy, only to lose her life in an Indian raid on her final settlement. The Governor gave also a lively account of affairs of state in which he had participated—notably the attempt to end a boundary dispute between Massachusetts Bay and New Hampshire back in the forties; and the difficulties in those days of establishing a firm monetary system, in a province that was perversely drowning its commerce in the bogs of a bottomless currency. When history brought him to refer to the period when it was his duty to attempt enforcement of the Stamp Act, the Governor spoke modestly of his own opposition to the measure—an opposition which he had been forced, as Chief Justice, to subordinate to the sacred duty of law enforcement.

66

At this point Lord Hemynge spoke up. "In London we were well aware of your efforts to secure compliance with that difficult statute. And Sir Francis Bernard gave me vivid accounts of the terrible suffering and loss inflicted on you by the mob that pillaged your house. By the way, it was not this house, was it?"

"No, my lord, it was my residence in Boston."

Lord Hemynge looked directly at him. "You carry the memory of such an offense with a notable forbearance, Governor."

Mr. Hutchinson bowed gravely. "My lord, I have learned that no property is repaired by bearing malice." He paused a moment. "Of course, no man could enjoy the memory that his life was so near to extinction as mine was on that occasion." He returned Lord Hemynge's look, full in the eye, with an air of challenge. It was as though he were demanding: "Who are you, that you do not disclose your official mission to me, the Governor of the Massachusetts? Why do you touch on our most serious affairs with a lightness that resembles nothing so much as mockery? A light attitude to the crisis of the town of Boston is improper. I, the Governor, have the right to judge what is proper in government of this town and province. There is my right of office—and there is my right of experience. More than any other bearer of the authority of the Crown, I have stood firmly against my own people when I have seen them to be in the wrong. What do you want of us, you powdered and belted earl?"

But if Mr. Hutchinson could resent the attitude of lightness he detected in the emissary of His Majesty's Government, he could not himself sustain for long the attitude of challenge to high, titled authority. At other moments in their intercourse the Governor showed signs of nervous uneasiness, impatience to have his curiosity satisfied, and even a touch of grievance that he should be so played with.

But Lord Hemynge had decided that he would not reveal the nature of his mission until he was acquainted with the ver-

67

dict of the jury and the sentence of the court in the trial of
the soldiers before the bar of justice.

The word was brought at an early hour of the evening by
Lieutenant Colonel Dalrymple, who rode out from the town on
horseback. He joined Governor Hutchinson and his guest in
the library of the house at Milton, where they had been most
comfortably settled before a blazing hearth.

"I must pay my respects in haste, your honor," the soldier
said. "Have you received the verdict?"

"No, sir, I have not. What is your report, Colonel?" The
Governor's extreme anxiety communicated itself to Lord
Hemynge.

"Six of our men are declared 'not guilty'! Two are found
guilty of manslaughter—Killroy and Montgomery. They
pleaded for benefit of clergy, which the court immediately
granted. The sentence was that they be burned in the hand
and then be released. Captain Preston stood by them. I had
him escorted by an armed guard from the island to take charge
of the released prisoners. I saw them safely aboard the boat,
off for the Castle again."

"Thank God—Thank God!" The Governor was very pale, and
actually bowed his head almost reverently. "Our hopes may
be restored."

Then, in a tone that grated on Lord Hemynge's ear as thinly
official, the Governor asked: "And the town? Did it seem
reasonably quiet as you came out?"

The Colonel came back at him sharply. "The town—God
forgive it—is quiet." He suffered an outburst of fury. "The
town is sniveling in quiet, God blast it!"

"How unlike true-born Englishmen," Lord Hemynge murmured.

Colonel Dalrymple made a terrific effort to control himself.

"I beg your indulgence, my lord—but what my officers and men have put up with from this town is beyond endurance. It is beyond imagining. I have sent off a message to General Gage requesting that this command be relieved immediately from duty in the port of Boston. This is the lowest duty in the British Empire. It is far beneath the deserts of two such honorable bodies as the 14th and 29th Regiments of Foot. Most of the 29th is already in New Jersey. I pray God *all* of us may be sent far away—to Canada, to Ireland, to India—to anywhere in hell but Boston!"

"Let me remind you, Colonel," the Governor said firmly, "that your regiments have been assigned here in accord with properly enacted decrees of the British Government. Their duty has been difficult and unpleasant. Such duty cannot be unfamiliar to them. They encountered trouble in its performance. They were falsely accused. They found able defenders in this town. Justice has been dealt to them."

The Colonel was silent, but not mollified.

Mr. Hutchinson went on: "Sit down, Colonel. Rest yourself a moment. I shall order some wine."

The Governor left the library. There was something abrupt in his movement, as though he had been uncomfortably shaken up by his passage with the Colonel.

Lord Hemynge spoke to the distressed officer. "I find in myself some understanding of your resentment of the town of Boston, Colonel. More than a few of His Majesty's ministers in London at this moment would be in complete sympathy with you."

The officer was touched by this. "Thank you, my lord. I must confess that in my opinion such sympathy would be the least of our deserts." His exasperation crept up in him again. "My lord, you don't know—"

"Yes, Colonel, I do—or at least I can guess. It's been a time of bitter trial. But now, by grace of God and English law—an awesome institution, but one that sometimes works amazingly —you are well out of it."

The Colonel took this in with some bewilderment. "Yes—I suppose we are out of the worst of it. But today, sir, at the end, I thought I should have to order Captain Preston to be put under restraint. It drove him mad to see his men 'burned in the hand' by this colonial court. He feels their wrongs deeply. And so do I, sir, so do I." The Colonel shook his head ruefully. "That young Preston—the finest officer I've ever had on my staff. Wasted—wasted. It is *not* justice!"

Lord Hemynge once more found it necessary to speak soberly and sincerely. "From what I have seen and heard since I have been ashore in this town, Colonel, I am convinced that you and your officers and men have done honorably by your duty. Yours seems to me just such a force as Mr. Pitt might have rejoiced in, in those great days when he guided Britain to victory wherever she was challenged and threatened. I shall see him when I return to England. It shall be my pleasure to speak to him, and to the ministers, of the honorable performance in difficult and irksome duty of the 14th and 29th Regiments."

This touched the soldier's "point of honor and pride of valor." That Mr. Pitt—the great Lord Chatham—should hear of their ordeal put a new face on it. The earnestness with which this unknown peer spoke gave Colonel Dalrymple a fleeting hope that the message might reach the great man, for once, without the official translation into terms that would give all credit to General Gage. There was a start of tears in his eyes as he muttered, "Thank ye, m'lord."

Lord Hemynge changed the subject. "Your men were fortunate in their counsel in court. This Adams defended them most capably."

"Yes, my lord—he did that."

"Do you mind, Colonel—I am very much interested in this question. Will he be well rewarded for this pleading?"

The Colonel puckered his brow. "Now, my lord—Preston has told me . . . he paid him first a retainer of a guinea, then five more as a fee. I believe there's been another eight guineas put down as a fee for the soldiers, also. I haven't heard of anything

70

more. Perhaps—I don't know." He turned apologetically to the peer. "Money is scarce with soldiers, you know, sir."

"Yes, I know. And with ministers, too, sometimes," his lordship said dryly. Now he had one more question in his mind, and submitted it to the officer soberly.

"Colonel, there is another piece of intelligence I should like to have about this case. If you are not at liberty to disclose it, please do not hesitate to say so. It is important to me to know whether the Acting Governor had anything to do with engaging Adams as defense counsel for your men. Can you tell me?"

The Colonel frowned. His expression suggested that he would make an effort to answer the question honestly—and that the answer could not be a simple yes or no.

"Last March, my lord, when we were in despair—Preston and his men were arrested by order of the Acting Governor, you know, as the civil magistrate for the town of Boston as well as for the whole province—of course I sought Mr. Hutchinson's advice. He gave careful thought to choosing counsel for us. He named Adams then, saying we ought to get him to close for us if we could. It was his idea that we go to Quincy first. Hutchinson seemed to know that the consciences of these Boston lawyers would acknowledge our right to be defended before the bar. He even guessed that Quincy would hold off agreeing unless Adams would engage for us, too. I must say his advice was good—that's exactly how it worked out. I suppose he knows the bar of this province well, having served as Chief Justice. But he warned me not to let anyone know that he had made such a suggestion. Therefore I must ask you to hold this communication in confidence, my lord."

"On my word, Colonel," the Earl assured him. But now he must not leave unresolved the crucial point. "Are you certain that the lawyer Adams could not have known that such a suggestion was made by the Governor?"

The Colonel faced his questioner honestly. "No men in our position would have dared to tell him, my lord, for fear that we should lose him."

71

Lord Hemynge felt that he had never heard a simpler nor a more candid statement spoken by an honest man.

"I am grateful to you for this information, Colonel," he said.

❦

Mr. Hutchinson returned to the library presently, followed by a servant with a tray bearing a bottle of wine and three glasses.

"Please pardon my delay, gentlemen," said the Governor. "A messenger arrived with a letter from my good brother Oliver. He was not able to send his tidings of the trial as promptly as we had planned. But it is as well that we had the news directly from you, Colonel."

The Colonel nodded an acknowledgment but said nothing.

The servant went out. Mr. Hutchinson filled the glasses, and handed one to each of his guests. Holding his own glass, he turned to Lord Hemynge.

"Both the Colonel and I are very close to the business of the day in Boston, my lord. Perhaps you would propose the toast for us?"

The three men were standing. Lord Hemynge smiled at the Governor and said: "To the triumph of Time and Truth!"

Once again Thomas Hutchinson boggled at his visitor's tone, this time at the very largeness of the prospect that opened before them. But he drank the toast with distaste, as the Colonel did with indifference.

The officer made his excuses immediately afterward, saying that he must rejoin his staff at Castle William that night. He put no warmth into his leave-taking of Lord Hemynge, as though he repented of having spoken out so plainly on civil affairs for which he had no relish. Mr. Hutchinson escorted him to the door, and returned swiftly.

He began to speak with a new flowing eagerness, even before he had resumed his seat. "We have come out of this whole bloody affair of March the fifth far better than I could have hoped, my lord," he began. "We should have been in a calamitous situation if the verdict had gone against the soldiers. They would of course have thrown themselves on executive clemency, and I should have been compelled to act. I do not see how I could have avoided issuing a reprieve, to give His Majesty time to review the sentence."

"And to what—or to whom—do you credit this fortunate outcome, your honor?" Lord Hemynge asked.

Mr. Hutchinson could not restrain a laugh. "To patience, my lord—patience on a monument. We have exercised patience to the point of exhaustion. But the tactic of delay and postponement was our only hope. It has rewarded us."

"Then the Royal Government of this province owes a good deal to your choice of the shrewd tactics—and to human patience. Possibly, also, to the earnest efforts of Adams and Quincy as counsel for the defense of the prisoners?" Lord Hemynge suggested.

"Oh, yes—to the counsel, too; we may as well admit it."

"It seems to me," said Lord Hemynge with a trace of sharpness, "that we might do better to proclaim it."

Mr. Hutchinson boggled again, in spite of his high spirits. "I do not follow your sense, my lord," he said.

"I mean that if the speech of John Adams had the effect on the court and the town that it had on me, we should be prepared to thank him generously for rendering the highest possible service to his country. My estimate would be that his advocacy of the soldiers in this trial has given to Massachusetts Bay and Great Britain alike, time in which to review their difficulties, and possibly to mend them. I have never heard a finer strain of eloquence than the lawyer Adams displayed yesterday in the courtroom. I only wonder whether the provincial government has within its bestowal any reward fitting for the measure of his service."

Mr. Hutchinson considered this for a moment. Then: "My lord, I have watched John Adams for a long time. Certainly he is an able advocate. From the start he has been too often allied with the dissidents—the fomenters of rebellion. Of course, he has never been the agitator, the outright rebel, that his kinsman, Sam Adams, is. But I have overlooked his peccadilloes, and as recently as two years ago I offered him a post as advocate general in the Court of Admiralty at Boston. The offer was made formally by Sir Francis on my recommendation through a trusted mutual acquaintance. Adams refused the post. We gave him time to reconsider, and renewed the offer. He refused it utterly. And he told Mr. Sewall, our intermediary, that to take the post 'would be to accept obligations and restraints' that he 'could not in honesty accept'! When you consider the care Sir Francis had taken to specify that there was no intent to put him under obligation, the reply was sheer impudence!"

The Earl expressed a becoming astonishment. "It would almost appear that he did not trust you, your honor," he said.

"Exactly! Exactly that!" Mr. Hutchinson exclaimed, with an incredulous laugh. Then the flavor of his visitor's speech struck him, and a frown of distaste appeared on his countenance.

"But I understand," Lord Hemynge went on blandly, "that this stubborn and ungrateful person has accepted an appointment—or is it an election—by the Town of Boston, to serve as its representative in the Legislature? Quite recently?"

The Governor nodded. "It was an election—quite by acclamation in the Town Meeting. It took place last June, some months after it was generally known that he had engaged to defend the soldiers." Mr. Hutchinson contemplated this point thoughtfully. Its meaning did not appear to be completely clear to him. "The truth is, my lord, that the town of Boston and her favorite so-called 'patriots' have in recent years resorted to perversities that are beyond accounting for. The best I can do is to ascribe them to the devious tactics of this lawyer's kinsman, Sam Adams. That man's bearing and his actions with respect to myself, as civil magistrate, and to Colonel Dalrymple, as military commander, immediately after the affair of March the fifth, constituted sedition of the most vicious nature. I

74

must confess to you, my lord, that I cannot understand why that treasonable conspirator permitted his kinsman to undertake the defense of the soldiers in the Superior Court of Boston. I should have expected him to make John Adams' continued residence in the town intolerable after such a commitment. Instead, we get the defense lawyer turning up in the lower house of the General Court as a member of the Boston seat— and such an election depends entirely on Sam Adams' approval. Of course, the hands of both Adamses have been busily engaged in the session of the General Court which I summoned this fall in Cambridge. Legislative effrontery has never been so brazen as in this session."

Lord Hemynge permitted His Honor to brood for a moment on his executive troubles with the legislature. Then he suggested mildly: "Even so, has it not been advantageous to the administration—that is, to the Royal Prerogative party in the province—to have a man identified with the patriot cause as chief counsel for the soldiers in the late trial? Or do I mistake the cause? Was the administration of the province perhaps sincere in its prosecution of the charges of murder against the soldiers? And is this outcome a most unhappy frustration of your hopes?"

"Oh, no, sir—we filed the charges against the military under compulsion, so to speak. The acquittal is a great relief to me, as I have said. And yet" —the Governor hesitated—"and yet it galls me to think that Sam Adams, too, may find some advantage in this very same result. I believe he does. But what advantage, I can't guess."

The Earl of Hemynge again felt constrained to give credit where credit was due. At this moment he could accord it to the Governor for speaking honestly of a baffling affair. He could accord it to John Adams for what he had spoken clear and loud in the courtroom. And to the Patriot party of the Massachusetts Bay colony, he could accord credit for—what? For heeding Sam Adams' mysterious generalship?

But he must tap the Governor again. "Tell me, sir, is Mr.

Adams—that is, John, the lawyer I have heard in action—is he considered a respectable man? Does he prosper in his activities at the bar?"

"He is generally respected for his ability. This is just, for he deserves it," the Governor conceded. "He is gaining a larger share of the most lucrative law cases every year." Now the Governor took on that spritely air that seemed to go with his awareness of secrets. "But he is due for a setback. I have it on good authority that the Patriots' shipping man, John Hancock, will take his law business out of Adams' hands very shortly, and give it to Samuel Quincy. This will be a blow to Adams' practice, I can tell you."

"I'm sorry to hear it," Lord Hemynge murmured.

Mr. Hutchinson, with the air of gloating over an adversary whom he had not defeated, but who was falling into bad luck providentially, went on: "Since you ask me for an estimate of this man Adams, my lord, I might sum it this way: in spite of enjoying some respect and some prosperity, he is a disappointing man—and a disappointed man."

"Is he properly wived?" Lord Hemynge asked bluntly.

If the peer's intent was to deflate the egotism of the Acting Governor, he succeeded. Mr. Hutchinson detested anything that resembled a gaming-room manner of speech with respect to matters affecting the sex and matrimony. The present question did not go down with him at all. "He is married, my lord," he replied, coldly.

"Who is his wife? Can you tell me something of the connection he made by his marriage?"

Though the Governor was offended by his guest's tone of levity, he was so well versed in the gossip of the colony that he could not resist the question.

"His wife was a Miss Smith of Weymouth—south along our coast. Her father is a parson out there in the Congregational Church. The Smith connection is fairly modest. The lady's mother, however, was a Quincy. You have observed her kinsmen in leading places—uh—on both sides, in the late trial.

This is an honorable family from the early days of the Bay colony settlement, and stems from an English line of some distinction."

"Have you ever made the lady's acquaintance?"

"No, I have not, sir," Mr. Hutchinson finished rather curtly.

"I hope that I may have the honor of doing so during my visit to this province," Lord Hemynge stated quietly. Mr. Hutchinson nodded, without interest in the prospect.

Lord Hemynge determined that it was time to open up a subject in which he was certain that Mr. Hutchinson's interest would be absorbed.

❧

"If it suits your convenience, Mr. Hutchinson, may I disclose to you the nature of the business entrusted to me by Lord North?"

The Governor bowed his head politely, and made no other reply. But there was a faint stirring of alertness perceptible through his whole person.

"The administration contemplates, with royal consent, the establishment of a North American peerage," the Earl went on quietly. "It is agreed that the dispensing of such honors is most urgent in the Massachusetts Bay colony, where settlement of issues is also most urgent. I am empowered to make a selection, secure an acceptance, and report the result of my choice immediately to Lord North. The nature and extent of the compact among parliamentary parties and factions is such that we may be assured that elevation to an earldom, of the person whom I shall have the honor to recommend, will follow."

The envoy paused, struck by the intensity of the blaze of eagerness flaming in the eyes of Thomas Hutchinson. The Governor could not restrain an expression of his emotion. "At last! An end to all the neglect we have suffered. And an earldom! We had never thought of anything more than a decoration. Why—even Sir Francis . . ."

Lord Hemynge was horrified. He hastened to extend his explanation. To be coolly factual at this point was the only way to be merciful. If the Earl had momentarily had a desire to punish the Acting Royal Governor for the exhibition of small and mean presumptions, he lost it upon seeing this exposure of a great one.

"The policy envisions that the honors shall be awarded to leaders among what may be called the 'Patriot party' in these colonies rather than the 'Prerogative party.' No man who has held an office within the appointing power of the Crown may be considered. The prohibition extends even to the smaller offices. We go directly to choose among leaders trusted by the people in the several colonies. Of course, we desire that the elected parties should be persons who have the rudiments, at least, of the bearing of gentlemen. If we may find that among the Patriot leaders, there are by chance some persons accustomed to wealth or to maintaining a position of consequence, so much the better."

Mr. Hutchinson's subsidence into a bitterness of shock and disappointment was accompanied by the loss of healthy color from his countenance. He managed to control a mixture of emotions which, for all Lord Hemynge knew, may have included rage. It was necessary to admire the strain of iron in the Governor's character that could bring him to utter his present question with no more than a suggestion of resentful distaste.

"Are the Royal Governors of these colonies to be consulted in this matter, my lord?"

"They are to be informed, sir," Lord Hemynge said, with what he knew must be an infuriating calm. "And they will be expected to respect the secrecy of the negotiation."

Thomas Hutchinson nodded curtly. "No doubt they will. And the Acting Governors, too," he added, nastily enough to win further respect from Lord Hemynge for his spirit.

The Acting Governor of the Massachusetts Bay, with the

passing of each moment, was regaining his self-command. Now he drew a deep breath and spoke with passionate sincerity.

"It is my duty to warn you that there is no virtue in this proposal, my lord. Flattery and honors will never serve to subvert the conspiracy of the disloyal, in this hour of extremity. Only the strongest and most forcible measures are called for, as Sir Francis and I have urged innumerable times. The colonials who are of this falsely designated 'Patriot party,' including those who have acquired wealth and fame in defiance of the law, are confirmed in their ways. Opposition to constitutional authority is the source of their profit. The 'Patriot party' is a party of rebellion. Its most honored trade is smuggling. You are in effect inviting a set of wild Wilkeses into the House of Lords." His own mention of the name of the shameless agitator brought a suspicion into the Governor's mind. "Is the Earl of Chatham back of this?"

"He has given his consent to the negotiation," Lord Hemynge said.

The Governor sought a little revenge. "Tell me," he invited, confidingly, "tell me—fresh from London as you are, my lord: is Chatham really insane?"

"Is he—what?" cried Lord Hemynge.

"Insane? You understand, my lord—we heard such odd tales of incapacity, government by the Countess—all sorts of things, during his late ministry."

"Let me assure you," the peer said icily, "that nothing could be further from his mind than insanity. His health suffers. But with that royal game he has no truck whatsoever." Edward Humbird knew he protested too much. Chatham had certainly been profoundly "disordered," if not deranged, during that terrible failure of a second ministry.

"Thank you, my lord," said the Governor. "You set our minds at ease."

"Oh, I am certain that is the purpose of all the communications from the ministry to the Royal Governors," said his lordship cordially. Then, more seriously: "With respect to your expressions concerning the present proposal, your honor, I must admit that we are aware of its hazards. Nevertheless, as you yourself indicate, the situation is desperate, and we resort to this as to a desperate measure. When we have established a set of North American peers-designate, as we may call them, we shall work with them to establish a system of boroughs and borough representation for America in the Parliament. This is a recognition of some justice in America's pitiful cry for representation before taxation."

"I must protest, my lord—not pitiful! Never pitiful! Perverse, combative, rebellious, wrongheaded—and, if you ask me, insincere. They do not really want it. What about their holy charters, or the proprietorships in some cases, and these sacred General Courts or Houses of Burgesses, or whatever the various legislatures are called? Even Town Meeting here in Boston! Do you think they'll give those up for representation *with* taxation?" With an air of great certitude, the Governor ended: "Think again, my lord."

Lord Hemynge privately was more shaken by these questions and warnings than he was willing to confess even to himself. "We are perfectly aware, Mr. Hutchinson, that these negotiations present difficulties. As to the sacred institutions you mention, the colonial peers and commoners in the Parliament itself shall advise us on their best disposition." Lord Hemynge looked piercingly at the Governor. "Do not forget, sir, that the honors, the elevations, are remarkably handsome."

Thomas Hutchinson was not likely to forget that. First impressions made as strong an inroad upon his consciousness as upon any man's. But his armament was not yet reduced.

"I cannot fail to observe your interest in the Adams connection—particularly in John, the lawyer, of Braintree and Boston, my lord." He paused.

Lord Hemynge was intensely curious. "Yes?" he prompted.

The Governor frowned, and spoke with a more patently sincere concern. "My lord, they are a touchy race."

80

Lord Hemynge smiled. "Titles—peerages have gone to persons of a 'touchy' family strain before, your honor," he reminded his host. Then he rose to take his leave.

Mr. Hutchinson assisted him, summoned his coach, and the pair stood for a moment, rather silent, in the hall.

"I must venture a thought, my lord," the Governor finally suggested. "If your mission is one that must be carried through, I cannot forbear recommending that you look closely into the Quincy connection. It is quite 'patriot' enough for Chatham, I'm certain. Sober, steady, handsome—able men in many respects, and women of fine breeding and grace."

"Thank you, Governor, for your friendly advice," Lord Hemynge said. "But it occurs to me that Samuel Quincy, Esquire, has just completed a service for the Crown in the prosecution of the troops charged with murder in the 'Bloody Massacre.' And, as you have observed, sir, I am interested in the Adams connection, touchy or not. Thank you again, Governor, for your most gracious hospitality."

With a brief farewell from the Governor in his ears, Lord Hemynge stepped into his coach and began to move toward Boston.

Mr. Hutchinson returned to his pleasant library. He stood before the fire for some minutes, kicking absently with the toe of his shoe at a stout log, then at his finely wrought brass tongs and shovel, and he traced the arch at the base of one of the gleaming andirons. At first he was frowning. Gradually his face relaxed. Finally he smiled.

It is entirely possible that for the first time in his excessively distinguished career, he was doing full justice in his mind to the Adams connection.

Part Two

6

LORD HEMYNGE, SEATED THE NEXT MORNING AT A HANDSOME desk in the library of the house in which he was lodged, wrote his signature with a flourish. He pushed what he had written across to Tompkins, who was perched atop a small library ladder.

"Read it, Tom," the peer ordered.

Tom did so, mumbling bits of it aloud.

"To John Adams, Esquire:

"Sir.

"As a lately arrived Visitor in the Town of Boston, it has been my Privilege to observe a Part of the recent Proceedings in the Superior Court of this Town. I should be loath to return to London without making the Acquaintance of yourself, Sir, and without having had the Privilege of some Conversation with you regarding that Trial. I make so bold as to request that you name an Hour when I may have the Honor of waiting upon yourself, Sir.

"Yr most Obedient Humble Servant,
"EDW. HUMBIRD, 6TH EARL HEMYNGE"

Tompkins looked up. " 'Twill do, milud."

But the Earl needed more reassurance. "Then he will receive me? There's no doubt of it?"

In another mood, Tompkins might have been tempted to cackle on observing such diffidence in his great patron.

"They will be polite, milud," he assured the Earl. "They will 'receive' you. 'Tis certain, milud."

Lord Hemynge accepted this as good authority.

"One more question, Tom." His lordship paused. "You know my purpose." He directed a severe gaze at his servant. He had never actually reported to Tompkins in words the precise nature of his mission. He was convinced that Tompkins was aware of it, however. Under his scrutiny, Tom held a motionless, expectant attitude, neither confirming nor denying his master's assumption. This satisfied Lord Hemynge that the discreet creature knew everything. He put the question to him: "Are we on the right track?"

Giuseppe Tompkins had the grace to feel honored by his patron's confidence. He had tried honestly to earn it, and his own belief was that he had. For six months he had immersed himself in the club, tavern, and street life of Boston, absorbing the feelings and opinions of the town, studying the reputations of its leaders. One of the first manifestations he had encountered had been a groundswell of resentment against John Adams, for undertaking the defense of the soldiers. He had seen this feeling mysteriously reduced by some apparently silent manipulation under the fascinating, shaky hands of Sam Adams, the beloved brewer—so reduced that the lawyer's election to the Boston seat in the legislature had soon gone through the Town Meeting with overwhelming approval. Tompkins had sensed that these reversals centering about the rocklike but rather melancholy figure of the colonial lawyer would be just the thing to engage the interest of his lordship. In his devious but not fundamentally dishonest way, he had wagered heavily on John Adams. His master's course in Boston had proved to him that he had chosen well. Naturally enough, he felt a certain elation. He took a deep breath.

"In my 'umble opinion, milud, we be on the right and only track."

Lord Hemynge had a flash of appreciation for Tom's dogged

devotion. "Thank you, my dear boy," he muttered. Then he frowned, turned again to the business of doubting. "But are we sure we are not overlooking anything? This—ah, this—what did Hutchinson call him: 'the Patriots' shipping man, Handcraft'—no, 'Hancroft'?"

"Hancock, milud."

"Yes, that's the name. Why don't we look *him* over before we go too far with Adams?"

Tompkins had a sinking of the spirit. He chose his words not merely with care, but with his old Covent Garden artfulness. "Perhaps *you* should, milud," he began. "Johnny Hancock be very well liked along Ship Street and Fish Street. His pounds would serve him well. He be very shrewd in the nursing of 'em along, milud. He be deserting Johnny Adams right now, the talk goes, to place his law business with Sam Quincy—a very wise move, they do say, milud." He paused a moment. "But his voice, his tongue—" He shook his head ruefully.

"Yes?" his lordship prompted. "What about them? Doesn't he talk?"

Tom's expression was a combination of the wry and the troubled. "That's just it, milud; sometimes he do. And there be some as says to hear it is to hear an echo."

Lord Hemynge must challenge this. "An echo of what—of whom?"

"Of *Sam* Adams, milud," Tom finished meekly.

His patron reflected a moment. He took Tompkins' point to be that Hancock was no orator, depending on the "other" Adams for his drift. Then the contrasting picture came before his mind's eye, and what must be the totally contrasting sounds of utterance found his remembering ear—John Adams standing grim and firm beneath the bench, sturdy, doughty, indomitable, affirming to the world:

"I am for the prisoners at the bar . . ."
"Some call them shavers, some call them geniuses . . ."
". . . churchquakes and statequakes in the moral and political world . . ."

85

"There is no occasion for the magistrate to read the riot act . . ."

"They are wretched conservators of the peace!"

His lordship turned again to his faithful servant, his mouth slightly watering. "I must have a man who can talk!" he cried.

"Then Johnny Adams is our only hope, milud," said Tompkins with a sober gravity that completely disguised his exultant feeling of "I've won!"

The Earl of Hemynge rose. "Take the note to him, Tom. Ask him to give you a reply."

Tompkins knew well the modest lodging in Brattle Square that housed John Adams, his good wife and children. Tom's friends in the Sons of Liberty had often accompanied Sam Adams in his walks to his kinsman's house to take—not tea, which was under the ban of Boston's proud nonimportation agreement as being improperly taxed by the British Parliament, but coffee or chocolate. Sam used to turn them off at the door, warning them good-humoredly that his cousin's house didn't have space to accommodate them all. But Tompkins had noticed that neither the master nor mistress of the house, when they happened to open the door to receive their expected visitor, ever looked with any cordiality of interest upon the Liberty crowd. The house was obviously small—but neither Mr. nor Mrs. Adams wished it were large, at least in so far as Tompkins could read the expressions of their faces upon those occasions. Now he knocked on the door that he had seen Sam Adams enter several times. A servant girl presently opened the door.

"I have a letter for Mr. Adams," Tom said. "An answer is requested. I am to wait for it."

The woman invited him to step into the small entry. "I do

not know— The doctor is here. I'll take the letter in to Mrs. Adams."

She left Tompkins alone, moving along a narrow passage. The entry was cut off from view of any other room by a winding staircase. Tom could hear that the girl tapped on a door, and there was a brief exchange of question and explanation, two women's voices. Then there was a stillness after the servant had moved on to the back of the house.

Presently John Adams came out of the room to face the messenger.

"You are the bearer of this?" he asked briskly, indicating the open letter he carried in his hand.

"Yes, sir," Tom answered.

"I have a visitor just now," the lawyer said. "I do not wish to take time to write a message. I shall send a note by hand later in the day."

"Yes, sir," said Tompkins. "Unless you wish to entrust a message for his ludship to me, by word of mouth. He wishes only to know a day and hour that would suit, that he might wait upon you."

John Adams looked at him rather sharply. "You are—his lordship's clerk?" he asked.

Tompkins was eager to accept the designation. It struck him as wonderful that his literacy should have been so quickly guessed and acknowledged by a colonial orator who might soon be more than that. "And secretary, sir," he added with a professional air.

"Then will you be so good as to tell the Earl of Hemynge that I am not engaged in business this afternoon? He has only to stop here at his convenience today—or tomorrow forenoon. Do you suppose this will suit?" Mr. Adams spoke with a touch of harshness that suggested a certain distaste for the transaction.

"It will suit perfectly, I'm sure, sir, Mr. Adams. I shall repeat your message immediately to his ludship. I daresay you may expect him to wait upon you today." Tom bowed.

"Very well." Mr. Adams was curt. He opened the door.

Tompkins, with an air of modest graciousness upon him, stepped through, down the stoop, and into the street. He turned to proffer another bow, but the door had been closed behind him.

John Adams returned to the parlor of his home. The persons whom he had left there were his wife and the Boston physician Joseph Warren. Seated, they watched him with expressions of concern when he rejoined them.

"You see, John," the doctor said, "there is such a thing as engaging in too much business. Here you are today, indisposed, with an ill digestion—yet when you most need a day of rest you are continually interrupted by messengers. Always, more business in the courts. You are doing too much. This trial—the General Court at Cambridge. You must learn to refuse solicitations of your time."

John Adams took the chair most distant from the hearth. There was no cheer in his expression. "The town of Boston itself has been in a fever these two—most of these ten years. Why don't you prescribe peace and quiet for the town, Doctor?" he asked.

Abigail spoke up. "That's a fair question, John." She turned to the doctor. Delicacy prevented her speaking her thought. But at this moment she longed to warn her husband against the danger of continuing his present course—the danger that his nerves, his mind, his health should suffer such a collapse as had been visited upon his and Dr. Warren's great friend James Otis—the first lawyer of the province, once a leader in the House of Representatives. Mr. Otis was become now an unstable, shattered person, often crazed by drink, almost a liability to the town in its time of stress. He had lately been beaten brutally in the street by some wretched minion of the customs service. No, Abigail could not warn her husband to beware the example of James Otis, not at this moment in Joe Warren's presence.

But the doctor scented the trail of her thought.

"I wish I could order a regimen of peace and prosperity for the town," he said. "For the sake of Mr. Otis—and for your sake, John. For our wives and children, for our friends. Perhaps now—if they withdraw the soldiers from the Castle, as they have taken them from the town—perhaps now it is just possible things may settle down somewhat."

John Adams didn't even look up. His fingers drummed on the letter he had placed on the table beside his chair. "You think that possible? With Hutchinson's messages coming regularly to the Legislature? With our House summoned to Cambridge instead of to Boston, where it rightfully belongs—on some pretext of its being 'the King's pleasure'?" The scorn in his tone was rough.

Abigail could not endure it. "Tell him, Doctor," she begged, "tell him what you were just saying to me."

Joseph Warren shrugged his shoulders and smiled faintly. "It's the last advice I want to give you. But if you value your health and your ability to maintain your energy, you had better retire for a time from business in Boston. You should follow a slender diet for this nervous indigestion. You should refuse all participation in public business." He stopped. It was clear that he had not said all that was in his mind. It was almost as though he had interrupted himself.

John Adams had heard him gravely. "Of course, I must pay serious attention to what you say. For the sake of my family, mainly. But"—now it was from courtesy that he avoided looking directly at his friend—"it can be made very difficult for a man to refuse to take part in the burning concerns of his country."

Dr. Warren took it in. "The reproach, if it is one, is in very

89

soft terms, my friend," he said with a gentle ruefulness. "I know that your cousin and I have been the first to press you to join in the public business when it becomes most troubled and distressing. No doubt we shall run to you tomorrow for new drafts to refute Hutchinson's legal perversities. Perhaps this confession tells you how urgent I consider my prescription. The only thing for you to do is—go to Braintree." He rose to leave. Crossing the room, he paused to rest his hand for a moment on John Adams' unresponsive shoulder. "I mean it, John. You are too valuable to us to be risked. We must see you restored to health and spirits."

John Adams did not move. Abigail in concern caught Dr. Warren's eye, and quietly went out of the room with him to usher him from her home.

She was back in an instant, all anxious and solicitous. "John, my dearest, are you worse?"

He stirred from his most unusual lethargy, almost irritably. "No, no—if anything, I'm quite well." He made an impatient motion of his head, as though to shake off the intentness of her gaze.

"John," she began a little defiantly, "you are to have a cup of tea." Seeing that this had brought to life a spark of indignation that in him was characteristic at least of better health, she prevented his protest. "No, not a word. These are ancient leaves I hid away in a canister, oh, months ago. It may or it may not be contraband. I don't care. You need a cup of tea, and you shall have it. And later you must lie down—you shall sleep."

Her husband evidently decided to pass over the tea controversy. Instead of taking up debate on that issue, he handed her the letter that had reached him a quarter of an hour earlier. "What is this?" she asked. "More business?"

"Read it," was all he said.

She did so rapidly. Her eyes had scarcely taken in the signature when an expression of amazement spread over her face.

"Good Heavens!" she exclaimed. "Now what on earth can *he* want?"

90

Something after two o'clock in the same day Lord Hemynge presented himself at the house in Brattle Square. He was admitted by the servant girl, who relieved him of his greatcoat and hat and hung them on pegs against the staircase, then ushered him into the small parlor. Mrs. Adams, alone in the room, rose to greet him. The servant did not announce him.

"I understand that you are Lord Hemynge, sir, and that you wish to see Mr. Adams on business."

"I do seek the pleasure of making Mr. Adams' acquaintance, and your own, ma'am," the peer replied, "but I may not claim that my purpose today is business."

"You are welcome here, my lord," Abigail said formally. "My husband will join us in a moment." She had decided to make no reference to John Adams' slight physical indisposition, but an impulse now swayed her from her intention. "He has been somewhat fatigued by excessive labors of late."

Lord Hemynge recalled that he had inquired of Mr. Hutchinson whether the Boston lawyer, Adams, were "properly wived." He felt now that after this mere exchange of greeting with Mrs. Adams, he was far better prepared to answer his own question than the knowing Governor had been. Mrs. Adams was handsome, graceful, kind, and was clothed not so much in the pleasingly modest grey-colored gown she wore as in a raiment of lovely dignity. It was not lost on Edward Humbird, that rather casually married master of Hemmingcourt, that this wife to a colonial lawyer, like the splendid Countess to the Earl of Chatham, considered her husband's well-being the matter of first importance in her life. Such women, wives, were rare and noticeable in society.

"I have myself been a witness to some of Mr. Adams' distinguished labors in the court of justice, ma'am. Such services must indeed bring on fatigue," Lord Hemynge said soberly. His intent was sympathetic, but even so Abigail glanced at him with a momentary doubt.

91

Then Mr. Adams was heard descending, and he joined them. Abigail saw that he was much refreshed by his rest.

"John," she said, with a touch of pleased confidence in her tone—it was the improvement in her husband's color that raised her spirits—"here is Lord Hemynge. My husband." She turned toward the visitor, with a little smile that had a pleasing pride in it, bowing her head slightly.

The men formally acknowledged each other's presence, and John Adams seated his guest beside the hearth. Abigail too sat down on a chair close to a window that overlooked a small, neatly tended garden. She had received an impression from the visitor's first words that he wished her to remain in the room rather than to retire as she did when it appeared that gentlemen in her house wished to speak of business to her husband.

She was glad to remain. The appearance, manner, speech, and dress of the Earl of Hemynge pleased her. He was a tall and well favored man, but somehow by courtesy managed not to make John Adams appear short-statured. His carriage and movements were elegant and easy. His facial expression was good-humored, and made her feel that he took her to be a person of good humor, too. His speech was without excessive London affectations.

Ah, but his dress! The French grey coat, with its facings of velvet; the multiple rows of stiff lace ruffles at wrists and throat; the scarlet satin waistcoat; the buttonholes wrought with gold, the gold-basket buttons; the smoothness of the breeches and stockings; but most of all, at head and foot, the perfection of the tight-fitted wig, the best fitted she had ever seen, and the shine of the great gold buckles on the perhaps also tight-fitting shoes!

. Mrs. Adams had sometimes thought that the elaborate grooming of a great nobleman turned out in flawless London dress would surely be a target for scorn. She found a little breathlessly today that such was not the case. If anything, her visitor's splendid aspect invited her good dispositions in his favor. And it was impossible for her to ignore the fact that the meeting between herself and the peer had been a success of that valuable kind, the mutual.

"May I say at once that my reason for seeking your acquaintance, Mr. Adams, is my wish to express the deep satisfaction with which I followed your plea in defense of the troops of the 29th Regiment, in the court, two days ago," Lord Hemynge said.

John Adams inclined his head very slightly. "The argument was submitted in behalf of justice, and in no other cause, my lord," he replied, with an unrelaxed severity.

"I am certain that was the case, sir," his lordship agreed. "And I am convinced, from hearing your summations of evidence, that justice was done—that the verdict is proper. I am here briefly on a mission for the government, Mr. Adams. On my return to London I shall take great satisfaction in reporting to the ministry that Boston justice is true English justice"— his lordship improvised an amendment hastily, recalling that the province claimed to be oppressed by English injustice—"at its best."

But he was not swift enough to elude Mr. Adams. "English justice has been obstructed too often lately—in Boston, and in London, too, I understand."

"That is true, Mr. Adams," the peer conceded, "in spite of the efforts of such men as Lord Chatham, Lord Rockingham, Mr. Burke—and, I may say, yourself and Mr. Quincy, sir."

John Adams' composure was shaken slightly by the direct tribute. The bracketing of his own and Josiah Quincy's names with those of the greatest Whigs struck him as extravagant. He was afraid of flattery.

But Abigail was unshaken. "It is pleasing to hear *you* speak so justly, my lord," she said honestly.

"And, let me assure you, in all sincerity," Lord Hemynge insisted. "Mr. Adams, you know as well as I do—as well as Lord Chief Justice Hale, or Chancellor Fortesque, whom you cited so effectively in your argument—that the course of English justice has never run smooth. From Magna Charta on, it has

93

ever had to flow through obstructions thrown up by perverse subjects."

"And rulers," Mr. Adams tossed in grimly.

"And rulers." The Earl accepted it, with a bit of a mental gasp. He wanted to keep Royalty out of this. It had its own perversities, but it was constitutional; some still thought it was of divine origin, and in the present case it was irremovable. Not even the Bostonians were contemplating regicide. "No doubt we may include the legislatures, the lawmakers, among those who sometimes make the course of justice difficult. Surely it is the errors of the British Parliament more than any other factor that has foisted injustice upon the English subjects in North America. The leaders in Lords and Commons are deeply concerned by the results of those errors which we see all about us today. They are prepared to acknowledge past mistakes. They seek to amend the failure of understanding between Old England and New. Indeed, my own mission to Massachusetts Bay, at the instigation of the ministry, is part of a determined effort to supply more accurate intelligence between the British government and this province."

Mr. Adams looked at the peer fair and square. "Since you speak of the failure of understanding between Old England and New, my lord, you will excuse my speaking plainly of what may appear a very provincial ignorance. But the exchange of information between Boston and London is so faulty that we of this town are not aware of your office."

The Earl of Hemynge recognized that he was being asked, "Who are you?" He rather enjoyed the sensation.

"I hold no office in the government, sir. I have been commissioned by the ministry to conduct a negotiation whose nature may not yet be disclosed. I am directed also to report my observations of the condition of this colony to the ministry on my return. There is no doubt that the ministry and I are fortunate in what I have observed. For I arrived in Boston in time to attend the closing of the defense for the troops of the 29th Regiment of Foot in the Superior Court of this town."

John Adams still did not have enough evidence to speak out with his usual candor. But it was enough for Abigail.

"Boston must rejoice, Lord Hemynge, that a report of this great triumph of justice in our courts shall reach the ministers from one who witnessed it himself." She spoke with a fervor that was controlled only by her fine pride. "For we have not had confidence that our case has been presented fairly to the government by—by those whose duty it is to report our condition officially. Boston has been injured deeply, my lord. And those who should be our warmest and most devoted advocates —they only fail us." She checked herself, and was thankful that she had not burst out with a more direct accusation of "the Governors—the Governors—the Royal Governors!"

From a reflective stillness, John Adams raised his eyes directly to meet Lord Hemynge's gaze. "That's fairly enough spoken, sir," he said firmly.

"So I hear," said the Earl of Hemynge, bowing slightly toward Abigail. "What I must communicate to the ministry is impressive. I must report that the trial of the soldiers was conducted with the utmost scrupulousness under the observation of a populace whose passions were much inflamed against the prisoners. I must report that the defense presented in their behalf was a noble argument that was closely attended. And the verdict shall speak for itself." Now the peer looked straight at John Adams, as though to warn him that he must be prepared to hear what he did not like to hear. "My greatest satisfaction shall be in reporting my observations to Lord Chatham. I shall inform him that there is eloquence in Massachusetts Bay worthy to be matched with his own, and that I have heard it with my own ears. I must report to him that this power is owned by John Adams, Esquire, of the Boston seat in the Massachusetts Bay Legislature."

The Earl paused a moment, noticing that the subject of his projected report to Lord Chatham was flushed and uncomfortable. But he knew that the kind of discomfort he was creating in that man's breast was of a nature that John Adams or any other lawyer could well stomach. "I wonder if you men of Boston are aware of the extreme importance of the gift of eloquence in the councils of state, Mr. Adams? He who would sway the Senate needs much of it; he who would convince a court requires it; and he who would move the people to wise courses must have it at his command. The Earl of Chatham used his gift of eloquence to move the people, to sway the Senate, and to guide the armies and the fleets that saved and extended the British Empire ten years ago. The inspiration of his eloquence reached across the sea, and animated the true-born English of North America, making them favorite sons of our Nation. Since those great days, he has spoken out only rarely. His health has been shattered by the magnitude of his efforts. He came out of the sickroom to Commons, to support Lord Rockingham's motion for repeal of the Stamp Act. He dared to say, 'I rejoice that America has resisted.' He formed a government again four years ago, but was too much tormented by his sickness to lead it. In his absence, the errors of Bute, Grenville, Newcastle, Townshend, have been compounded again. Only now, while his ministry has fallen and been replaced, is he sufficiently restored to take the seat in the Lords which he so nobly has earned. His eloquence again is heard—his strength, which he uses for justice in government, will be felt. America will know again that her friend is abroad. Of course, the old Parliamentary factions are afraid of him; he has fought them all as he felt he must. He is against tight alliances of party and faction, you know. He is for government by measures, not by men. But the measures—and he, too—need strong allies among men." Lord Hemynge paused. Then he finished quietly. "He shall find them—in England and America."

The Earl's commentary on Chatham had given John Adams an opportunity to recover from the flattery that his visitor had begun by voicing. "Of course, his illness has been a calamity for Great Britain—and for these provinces, too," he said gravely.

"I perceive that you are aware, sir," Abigail began, "that William Pitt is still warmly admired in North America. Have you heard that a statue has been erected to him in the port of Charleston, in Carolina? There is a Fort Pitt in Pennsylvania. And there is a Pitt Street in Boston." She added the last with a touch of modesty.

"He has spoken the wish that he might leave England to dwell in North America," Lord Hemynge stated. "He would do so out of his great respect for the spirit of liberty that flourishes in this continent."

John Adams smiled. "I am sure that he would be cordially welcome among us, wherever he might choose to settle."

"And his lady, too," Abigail said.

"Unfortunately, Lord Chatham conditioned such a move on his part by the proviso that ten years must be removed from his age," Lord Hemynge concluded.

"Perhaps our Massachusetts air would do that for him, my lord," Abigail suggested, smiling.

"He deserves to breathe it, Mrs. Adams," the Earl said lightly. "He has spoken in behalf of this province many times, in the House of Commons."

This touched something in John Adams. "Yes, my lord, he has spoken in our behalf. Many people in this province will receive in good part the opinion that he advocates *our interest* in the British Parliament. But no one can maintain that he *represents us.*"

Inwardly, Lord Hemynge felt a surge of confidence. The right road was opening before him. Mr. Adams himself had introduced the subject of representation. He now presented to his host, this member of a touchy race, his most earnest and respectful expression: "Lord Chatham himself would not pretend that he *represents* this province, Mr. Adams. He has denounced the doctrine of 'virtual representation' of the colonies, which was forwarded by the Grenville party in the Stamp Act time, in the most contemptuous terms. We should find few to defend that doctrine in the Parliament today. Lord Chatham's argument demolished it. A new view of the deserts of the English subjects in the North American colonies with respect to representation is taking hold. The lawmakers of England—King, Lords, and Commons—are ready to give a respectful hearing to the North American view. Boston's scrupulous dispensing of justice in this late cause, so difficult, so perilous, will beyond doubt be a deciding factor in bringing about overtures of conciliation from the British Parliament to the English colonial legislatures on this shore. In fact, measures are today in preparation to effect such a policy."

Mr. Adams and his wife were giving the most rapt attention to their visitor's statements. To Abigail, indeed, it seemed proper that her husband's great plea for justice should have become a determining factor in a fair and equitable settlement of the differences between England and America. John Adams, in his fatigue, heard his guest's previsions with attention—and skepticism. Yet both of them had been deeply absorbed in the prospect opened by Lord Hemynge's forecast. They both suffered something of a shock when he rose suddenly.

"I must take my leave," he said. "I have only a few more days in Boston. I need urgently to receive a sane communication of the views of the Boston seat with respect to representation. I cannot properly ask you to take time to enter upon such a discussion today. But I do humbly ask that you—you and Mrs. Adams—dine with me in my lodging in Marlborough Street tomorrow. Your acceptance will be a great favor to me."

The Adamses, rather dazed, had slowly risen to their feet, to stand with their guest. When the invitation was given, their glances met—John's full of a sober consideration; Abigail's one of surprise, in which a twinkle of eagerness danced. She was hopeful, but tried not to show it; and certainly she concealed her dread lest John utter a hasty or sharp refusal.

Now to her pleasure he spoke out quite affably. "Thank you, my lord. We shall be most pleased."

Lord Hemynge bowed, and moved into the hall. While Mr.

Adams assisted him with his coat and hat, he identified his lodging more specifically as the Province House.

Then he was gone.

"Now we know the answer to your question, Abigail," John Adams declared, on rejoining his lady. He was showing more of good spirits than at any time since the late trial began.

"What question of mine do you mean?" she asked innocently.

"Perhaps it was rhetorical. When you read our visitor's note, you asked, 'What on earth can he want?' "

"So I did. And I still want to know. But I can see it does no good to ask you. You don't know, either."

"Indeed I do."

"John! You can't have had a whispering match out on the doorstep. He's made no show of purpose here. Very well, then. What does he want of us?"

"He wants us to dine with him tomorrow."

"Oh," she said gravely, "so he does." Then she laughed, but quickly restored sobriety to her face. "I can do better than that."

"Excellent! What does my oracle-woman say?"

"He's going to be the new Governor," she announced positively.

He was really startled. "By heaven—you are a wise one!" They looked at each other, speculating.

"It could be," John Adams murmured, "it could be you are right."

They burst out laughing. They sat down together at the hearthside, laughing.

"And we are the first to receive him," Abigail gasped out.

"Oh, no—no! Surely not!" John was firm. "He's been to see Hutchinson first."

They hadn't had such a good laugh in years. And it wasn't over yet. Abigail was bursting with an amendment.

"That's right." She finally managed to get it out. "But he didn't *tell* him!"

"He didn't tell *us*, either," her husband reminded her rather weakly.

"I know," she moaned, wiping a tear. "But we kept our wits about us. He couldn't deceive us!"

They were off again. When she thought they were sober enough, Abigail tried to apologize. "My dearest, I am sorry to be so trivial. Do pardon me. But what does he—"

Once more they broke down. Then they were exhausted enough to face toward duty again.

"I must get my blue padusoy out for pressing and freshening," Abigail murmured to herself. She thought of that couple with whom they had shared their best hours in company, at Lynn—her sister Mary and her husband, Richard Cranch, one of John's greatest friends. "Sister Cranch will be so glad."

"Black broadcloth will solve my problems, I daresay. Just as it would Brother Cranch's, if he were concerned in this."

"I wish they were going too," Abigail said. She turned to him. "It will be a refreshment, John. One last engagement in Boston. Then back to the farm and the good life of Braintree. I'm going to hold you to that, John. I have Joe Warren to back me up."

The sickness he had suffered early that morning came to his mind and stirred uneasiness in him. "Yes," he began, "I suppose it must be. I'll be better out of Boston and her public business for a time." He ended decisively. "We all will."

This was such a great concession that she felt a pang of concern. "John, is there anything in this gentleman's visit that disturbs you? If there is, you know, we can properly send after him and refuse the invitation. We shall do just that, if this affair worries you at all. Have you heard anything about his business? Did you know he was coming to Boston?"

"I have heard Sam Adams mention some peer who was being sent over. Said he'd heard he was a Wilkes man, from somebody or other. Sam didn't seem to give it much weight. Neither do I." No—he did not. For surely Lord Hemynge was wanting in the *look* of a Wilkes man.

"All I want to know, John, is that you're easy about it," Abigail persisted.

"Well, my dear, there you are. I'm easy about it." He paused, and looked into the fire. "As a matter of fact, I'm curious about why this—this 'peer of the realm' comes to me."

When Lord Hemynge returned to the house in Marlborough Street, he was greeted at the door with an almost ceremonious formality by Tompkins. Such a manner, indeed, was the one cloak with which Tom could cover his extreme curiosity when the peer was deeply engaged in business and appeared to be in a reflective rather than a communicative mood. But on this occasion he was not to be tormented by a prolonged suspense. His patron beckoned him into the library.

"They will dine here tomorrow, Tom," the Earl began.

Tompkins could have given a cheer that might have sounded rather like a crow of triumph. But he was quick to take the tone of grave attention to business.

"They, milud?" he prompted.

"Mr. and Mrs. Adams," Lord Hemynge explained curtly. "I intend that they shall be offered a decent entertainment. Take that jug of Madeira from my hamper and decant it. There are some spices and bottled sauces in the same container. Take them out. See what we can use at the board tomorrow."

"Yes, milud."

"And Tom—my packet of music manuscript. Bring that down. I want some music for these people."

"And who is to perform it, milud?"

"Find me a spinet player and a fiddler here in this town."

Tom's eyebrows went far toward his stiff black pompadour.

"In this town, milud? For to perform proper-like tomorrow? They'd need to be sight readers of the best, milud!"

101

His patron looked at him sternly. "You've been here half a year, Tom, using your eyes and ears."

The consternation retreated from Tom's expression. "Oh, yes, milud." He was thoughtful. "There be a fiddler come to play for the fishery men over in the grog shop on Leverett's Lane, hard by Water Street. His ear is true, but how fast he be with his eye, that I do not know, milud."

"You can rehearse with him all night and all day, Tom—lead him with the flute or the hautboy. Play alongside him. How about the spinet?"

"Yes, milud, there be some young ladies . . ."

"No young ladies, Tom."

"There's a schoolmaster on Copp's Hill used to come down to the coffee shop in Hanover Street. . . . I'll see, milud. I seem to recollect he understood what to do on top of a bass."

"Find him and try him out. Or else whoever it is that teaches the young ladies. Get somebody, and rehearse him. If they pass muster, I'll give them a guinea apiece."

"They'll pass muster, milud," Tom asserted with a sudden confidence.

Lord Hemynge smiled. "And you, Tom—you'd better rehearse that Concerto in B-flat."

Tompkins blinked, then smiled. "Y'r servant, sir," he murmured with a certain complacency. Now he felt that the assignment entrusted to him by the Earl was sufficiently important to warrant his taking a liberty—that is, asking a question. "All this, milud, for just the two of 'em?" In spite of his assurance, he ended a bit shrill.

"We shall find, Tom," his master replied, "that Mr. and Mrs. Adams will make us a very full company indeed. In truth, the music is addressed to Mrs. Adams. Something in her aspect invites me to believe that she has an ear. Whether she has ever used it or not, I do not know." Lord Hemynge paused. He gave his head a slight shake, but seemed not to be able to throw off a conclusion he had reached. "She is one of the finest ladies I have ever seen."

Now Tompkins was alarmed. He tried to rescue the Earl from such a compromising extravagance. "In the North American fashion, so to speak, milud," he offered hopefully.

"In the English style, Old or New," Lord Hemynge declared firmly.

7

THE NEXT AFTERNOON AT FOUR O'CLOCK MR. AND MRS. ADAMS entered the hall of the Province House. A chill North Atlantic wind clamorously followed and overtook them and was cut off from its pursuit only when Aaron, the grave servant, closed the massive door behind them. While he assisted them in removing their wraps, Abigail noted with pleasure the clean warmth of the air that now surrounded her, the brilliant illumination from great candelabra, and the spaciousness that somehow gave importance to an arrival, invited people to fill it.

The deep blue color of her padua silk gown, with its adornment of a heavy golden lace about the shoulders and bodice, became her splendidly. There was a bright winter bloom upon her cheeks, and her smooth brown hair, capped with a delicate lace matching that on her shoulders, had a soft sheen that might have been envied by ladies whose attendants could spend hours in the brushing and dressing of petulant mistresses' locks. If in this evening Mrs. Adams was very close to being a woman of impressive beauty, she owed the appearance mainly to her own happy and confident spirits.

The habit she had of watching her husband for clues to his mood, the state of *his* spirits, she exercised now—but with an optimistic confidence that since she felt so well herself, all must be well with John. As the servant moved into the arch that commanded the great room of the house to announce them,

Abigail became aware that in addition to being warm and bright, the air of the noble hall was alive with soft, enticing sounds. They were faint, so that she could not distinguish a melody in the distant violin strain that floated to her eager ears from somewhere in the mansion. But the sound was sweet; and also, in a fashion that soothed her, it gave an impression of elegance and order.

She put out her hands to touch her husband's arm gently. "Do you hear, John?" she whispered.

But she did not quite reach him. He was uneasy again, as though convinced that of all places, here was the one where he had the least reason or desire to be. His expression was severe and forbidding, his doughty frame stiff. Once again Abigail exercised her great gift—that of being able not to feel repelled from the barriers of severity or even of harshness that her husband might raise against circumstances. She was capable of knowing that they were never raised against her.

Their names had been pronounced: "Mr. Adams . . . Mrs. Adams." The servant stood within the arch, waiting for them to pass.

Abigail threw a smile to her husband, inviting him to share her great pleasure in this moment. Then with a serene and modest air she passed through the arch, certain that John would be close behind her. Indeed he was, for he needed to be near her this evening. The servant withdrew, and Abigail stopped her progress after a few steps.

In entering the great room she felt that she had entered England. This sense made the fact that she saw a "redcoat" standing close to the hearth less of a shock than it must otherwise have been. As it was, the sight was enough to force her to break her advance, and to wait for the guidance that must come now from Lord Hemynge, who was swiftly crossing the room to her. She kept her gaze turned downward till their host had bent over her hand, and clasped the hand of her husband.

"You do me great honor," he was saying. "I hope that your

105

passage through the wind has not exposed you to too great discomfort."

"The breeze is no more severe than usual at this season," John Adams commented rather brusquely.

"Breeze? You give it a very gentle name, sir," Lord Hemynge said smiling, and turned to Abigail.

She was ready for him. "It is very pleasant to be greeted with the sounds of music in this warm interior, after breasting such a breeze, my lord." Her quiet and good-humored concurrence in her husband's name for the gales of winter struck Lord Hemynge as delightful.

"And if it pleases you, Mrs. Adams, we shall have more music within this shelter."

Abigail noticed now that the music had stopped. For on hearing the names of his guests announced, Lord Hemynge had signaled to Tompkins to have the players silenced. As a result of his confidence in Mrs. Adams' ear, he had insisted that she and her husband be greeted by the sound of music. He had hoped that she would comment on the fact. But if she had not done so, he nevertheless intended to offer her more music. Of this art he was a stubborn partisan.

Now Lord Hemynge led his guests toward the wide hearth, there to present to them the redcoat at whom Abigail had avoided looking. It was Colonel Dalrymple, whom she had seen in the courtroom, but never met. Her husband made a decent, but hardly a warm acknowledgment of a polite address from the officer who was, in effect, the "father" of his recent clients.

The host also made a brief introduction of his secretary, pronouncing both of his names: Giuseppe *and* Tompkins. Tom made a very gallant bow, in fact all but knelt, before Abigail, murmuring, "Y'r servant, milady!" and a rather less extravagant courtesy to Mr. Adams, "Y'r servant, sir." Then he retreated toward the musicians in the far corner of the room.

The sense of shock that had struck Abigail upon seeing the redcoat when she entered the room was touched with a sense of guilt. It was as though she were ready to acknowledge that "we should not have come here, on the invitation of a peer of the realm whose views with respect to the liberties owned by the English people we do not know." And her uneasiness was further complicated by the secret knowledge that her own eagerness to accept the invitation, though expressed by no more than a hopeful smile to John at the crucial moment, had somehow been decisive. If she had turned upon him an expression all gravity or chilled by a touch of disapproval, he might have found that his own instinct was to refuse. And so they should never have found themselves making part of a company that included the commanding officer of the occupying troops, in a house that certainly must have been furnished to this envoy from the ministry by the Acting Royal Governor of Massachusetts Bay.

But now as Lord Hemynge guided her to a chair some distance from the uncomfortably hot blaze, she saw that the Colonel was addressing her husband with the air of a sober man of business who had much on his mind, and that John at least was listening. Well, it could do a member of the Boston seat in the General Court no harm to hear something of His Majesty's military business from a responsible leader in that business.

And besides, the courtesy with which her host was caring for her own comfort, slightly shifting for her the beautiful chair which was exquisitely adorned by a design of flowers and small birds in needlepoint, was engaging her attention. He seated himself on a chair beside her. Again, his dress was so splendid! For this evening he was wearing a gold-trimmed coat of a deep wine color, its tails wired. The position they fell into when he seated himself, showing no sign of taking special care about them, was a detail that was not lost upon the twenty-six-year-old colonial matron who happened to be a daughter of the Quincys.

He addressed her in a confidential tone. "It gives me great pleasure to afford the Colonel an opportunity to express his

107

gratitude to Mr. Adams. He is a soldier with a profound respect for the institutions of civil law and government. He recognizes that while his own mission in Boston has been difficult, the service rendered by your husband in the Superior Court was even more so. To serve as counsel for the military in the late trial required the highest courage and integrity."

Abigail underwent a softening of her feeling toward the Colonel. "My husband's task certainly was not easy to accomplish. And—I suppose it may be difficult for a wise military leader sometimes to reconcile his duty with his understanding of justice," she conceded.

Lord Hemynge was startled by her capacity to extend his reference. "You speak with sagacity, ma'am. I myself learned something of the truth you have just uttered during some years of service in the Royal Navy."

It was Abigail's turn to experience a surprise. It was not easy to imagine this elegant personage seated beside her sailing the seven seas in one of His Majesty's bottoms. "Perhaps I presume too much, my lord," she offered modestly. "I could not speak from my own knowledge, of course. But there is much testimony." She hesitated and then intoned softly:

> " 'Captain or Colonel, or Knight in Arms,
> Whose chance on these defenceless doors may seize,
> If deed of honor did thee ever please,
> Guard them, and him within protect from harms.' "

Lord Hemynge's admiration was quickening. He found it necessary to study his lovely guest a moment before he replied. "The citation is sublime, madam," he began. "It is worthy of the genius of Mr. Adams in the court of justice. For it is known to me that he and his colleague go far beyond the claims of duty and justice to the points of honor and mercy."

The warmth of the peer's tribute forced Abigail to look toward the hearth where her dear husband stood in conversation with Colonel Dalrymple. What Lord Hemynge had said was true: her husband *had* displayed genius in the performance of his duty in the court of justice, and the power to move justice toward mercy with honor. But you could never have guessed that he commanded such powers, to look upon his severe visage now. And in secret she knew how a woman could love such a man the more for the very scruples that forced him to doubt his own genius, and by which he invited others to do so as well.

Lord Hemynge reclaimed her attention. "I could wish that Mr. Handel had made an air for those lines of Milton's that you spoke, Mrs. Adams. He did such a service for the *Samson Agonistes* and the *Allegro* and *Penseroso*."

"Is he living today, my lord?" Abigail asked.

"No, Mrs. Adams, he died twelve years ago. It was my great privilege to have made his acquaintance during the last years of his life."

Abigail recalled the pleasure she had received from the sound of the music she had heard on entering this house.

"That was a pleasant tune that we heard on our arrival here, my lord," she said. "I hope we may hear it again."

This was what the peer had been waiting for. "That is one of the dance movements, a minuet, from an opera of Mr. Handel's. Permit me to have it repeated for you, with the gavotte and tamborino that should follow it." He raised his head, gazing across the room. Tompkins recognized the summoning movement, and sped to his lordship's side.

"The *Alcina* movements, Tom—in order. And you take the recorder in the last one."

"Oh, yes, milud!" was the eager response as Tompkins turned quickly and went back to his professional companions.

Lord Hemynge made no attempt to interrupt the conversation of Mr. Adams and the Colonel. When the players began the minuet, Abigail could perceive almost immediately that it was the most beautiful melody she had ever heard. She threw one glance toward her husband, in which she tried to convey an urgent invitation to him to listen closely. She saw him look

109

for a moment toward the musicians, and then return his attention to the Colonel, who went on talking. Then her own attention was concentrated on what she was hearing. Her host, watching her, smiled with satisfaction. There was no doubt about it: she had an ear.

Tompkins was properly proud of the performance he had been able to secure from two obscure young men of Boston on short notice. Jem Thacher, the schoolmaster of Copp's Hill, had recommended to him that they obtain for the fiddle part a young coppersmith lately arrived from London to try his fortune in New England. Jenkins Dosset was his name, or the name that had been given to him in the foundling's home where he had been raised. His opportunity to learn music had come from an assignment as bellows-boy in an organ loft. His apprenticeship had been to a Liverpool coppersmith who liked sacred music, and the boy's talent had not been neglected. He was having some difficulty in getting himself launched in his trade in Boston, and the unexpected fee offered for this musical performance was a boon to him.

The *Alcina* minuet which had in its melody all the melting tenderness of a supremely graceful and courtly love song, was followed by a more robust gavotte, persuasive, friendly, immensely good-humored. This movement somehow maintained its health and its balance even when the tune played itself in one variation rather upside down or hind-end-to. It found a place for a pensive reflection after all, and ended with a reiteration of its bracing vigor.

"Now the tamborino," Lord Hemynge murmured.

Abigail felt the flattery of her host's concern that she should be properly instructed to follow the sequence of movements. And the tone of his prompting whisper suggested that what was to follow would be important.

She found it to be so. Her husband turned with surprise toward the players, and the Colonel broke off his argument. The Adamses' instruction in martial rhythms was confined to the drum beats and fife notes that had sounded oppressively in

110

Brattle Square opposite their own dwelling, during the parade and drill hours of the hated 14th and 29th Regiments, Colonel Dalrymple commanding. Neither John nor Abigail had ever confessed that those sounds were sometimes stirring, in spite of the fascination they had exerted on their son, John Quincy. But now a quick-step beat of march-time was plucked out of the modest spinet, the violin tossed out a tune that was quickly picked up by Tompkins, his eyes almost popping out of their sockets as he blew upon and manipulated the tiny recorder, stamping his foot steadily, *one, two, three, four,* while the flashing windnotes insisted that he was the company mascot, a drummer-boy's boy, double-timing wildly about the ranks of the sturdy marching troop.

Abigail began to laugh with delight; a bright flush rose to her cheeks; and when Tompkins had piped and stamped his way to the finish, she could not restrain the eager cry: "Oh, please—may we hear it once more?"

Lord Hemynge waved a signal for a repetition, and the tamborino flashed out again, at an even more breathless pace.

Abigail turned gratefully to Lord Hemynge. "So this is what the great Mr. Handel offers us, my lord? We can do with more of it in Boston."

"In my view we can have scarcely enough of it in London, Mrs. Adams." The peer rose from his seat and made her a slight bow. "But in any case, we shall have more of it for you this evening—in Boston."

The servant Aaron brought in a tray with a decanter of his lordship's Madeira upon it, and four glasses. Lord Hemynge moved to direct the servant in placing the tray and handing about the glasses which the host himself filled.

The Earl of Hemynge was perfectly aware that it was hazardous to invite Colonel Dalrymple, commander of the troops lately assigned to the occupation of Boston, to meet the

111

Adamses in a company assembled in their honor. But the peer's own regard for the good soldier was so warm that when Colonel Dalrymple waited upon him unexpectedly half an hour before the Adamses were to arrive, he took a sanguine view of the mischance and asked the officer to remain to meet his other guests. After all, as troop commander, the Colonel was in effect the client of the Boston lawyer. And since the man of law had most handsomely won a highly favorable verdict for that client, it seemed certain, in the Humbird sense of the appropriate, that mutual respect between the two must have held to a fairly high level.

His lordship exercised discretion, however. He invited the Colonel to remain for a toast, but not to dine. This limited gesture was received with innocent good will by the Colonel, who intended to return to his mess at the Castle. He had waited upon Lord Hemynge to deliver a piece of news he had this day received in a despatch from London. The Earl heard it with interest, and asked the Colonel to communicate it to Mr. Adams.

During the musical entertainment Colonel Dalrymple modestly engaged Mr. Adams in conversation. He spoke with honest gratitude of the conduct of the defense in the court, and praised Mr. Adams' presentation. The lawyer heard these compliments coldly, making the barest of polite acknowledgments.

Then the Colonel introduced his news. "We are notified today, sir, that Mr. Grenville has died in England."

John Adams turned a swift sharp glance upon the bearer of this report. But he made no comment.

The Colonel tried to prod him a bit. "Since Mr. Grenville's measures were of such concern to this province some years ago, sir, I must suppose his removal from the scene will be considered an event of importance?"

Mr. Adams stirred slightly in his cold impassivity. "I know little of the man," he said. "I must suppose that few of our countrymen here know any more. So long as he was alive, we should remember that he was the originator of the Stamp Act, and we should have been apprehensive lest he return to high

112

office with power to propose more measures of the kind. We had no other thoughts of him. To such friends as he had, his death will no doubt be a loss. To the rest of humanity, I must suppose that it will be of little moment."

Colonel Dalrymple, too, was a scrupulous man, but he found himself rather baffled to discover a reason for continuing the conversation.

Then the lively dance movement that had so charmed Mrs. Adams took the general attention. After it was repeated, Lord Hemynge proposed, as he had at Milton Hill, his high Handelian toast: "To the triumph of Time and Truth!"

Abigail, at least, was pleased by its elevated tone.

Colonel Dalrymple took his leave after that, and presently the Earl of Hemynge and his provincial guests sat down in their places at a table set with a gleaming silver service.

The repast was characterized by great abundance. Boiled fish, roast fowl—a golden goose—and baked pork formed its basis. Its accents were in the sauces and spices and the wines that had been brought to the table from his lordship's hampers.

Abigail felt some anxiety lest her husband forget Dr. Warren's advice to adhere to a slender diet, but she observed that he was exercising restraint. She wished too that she could lighten his mood, which still appeared cold even to moroseness. But she was easily distracted by the flavors of some of the delicacies, and finding her host willing to talk about them, she herself found that her own high spirits could not be quenched.

A chutney that Lord Hemynge politely commended as a sauce for the goose seemed to her especially delectable, and she asked him, with a happy interest, what it was.

"It is, I believe, one of the finest discoveries of the East India Company, ma'am," the peer informed her. "I dare not venture to guess all that it contains. I became acquainted with it at Stowe, the home of the Temple family, when a visitor brought it as a gift. Lady Chatham was there on a brief visit to her brothers. The Earl was out of health and unable to accompany her. The Countess savored the chutney, and asked her brother's visitor, lately arrived from India, what it contained. 'Very plain ingredients, my lady,' he told her. 'Ginger, peppers, cloves, cinnamons, onions, mangoes, and brandy.' Lady Hester looked to be in a state of alarm, and she said, 'Dear me, however shall I keep this from Chatham? He is so well disposed to all of our imports from India.'"

Abigail was charmed into a sympathy with the Countess. "What a pity," she said, "that such a delicacy must be kept from his lordship! But I suppose his lady must guard his health."

"She must—she does," Lord Hemynge went on. "And a difficult charge she has. I fear that Lord Chatham's appetite becomes all whims on the eve of an indisposition, or in the course of it. The great kitchens at Hayes Place must be kept fired at all hours, with an infinite variety of cookery in progress, in the hope that what will suit will be in readiness at the moment a fancy for it strikes him."

Abigail's sympathy with the Countess deepened. "His constitution then is so delicate?" she asked anxiously.

"On the contrary, Mrs. Adams, my belief is that William Pitt's constitution is one of iron, or it could not have endured under the enormous burdens he has subjected it to. The conduct of the wars was equal in difficulty to the labors of Hercules. The gigantic efforts required of the minister certainly weakened him. Since those years, he too frequently lacks the strength to purify his system by the relief of a gout. Instead, it remains suppressed and ravages him within. It is unfortunate, but the spices and brandies in such dishes as the chutney invite the dreadful inflammations without releasing them."

"How sad," said Abigail, "how sad that so great and good a man cannot enjoy the pleasures of his table without such disabilities! But has he really given over his interest in America for a new interest in India? You spoke to us only yesterday, my lord, of his thought of removing to America to live."

"I am certain that Lord Chatham will never forget America," her host reassured her. "But he has an inherited interest in

114

ndia. The Pitt family fortunes have been considerably engaged there since the days of his grandfather, Governor Pitt of Madras."

Both Mr. and Mrs. Adams found it difficult to think what it would be like to have family fortunes founded in enterprises in such a remote continent.

John Adams had a question. "I recall your saying that William Pitt's proposed removal to America was not contemplated seriously, on the ground that he is past a proper age for such a move. But may I ask whether it was thought that he might find occupation here worthy of his abilities? Or was this supposed a proper scene for superannuation for him?"

Lord Hemynge found himself so amused by the curiosity of one of the brace of Adamses as to the possible official disposition of the declining powers of a Pitt, a Chatham, in the American continent, that he had to impose a rigid control on his humor before he could answer with a becoming gravity. "Granting that the move we are discussing was never more than supposed, it might have been thought that a royal governorship of the province of Canada, which was secured for the Empire by Mr. Pitt's ministry, would offer a suitable occupation."

John and Abigail Adams had the same thought: No great man could be content in the role of a royal governor in North America.

But neither of them spoke the thought. Abigail's oracle of yesterday, suggesting that Lord Hemynge himself might turn up as the new royal governor of the Massachusetts Bay, had been recognized as frivolous. Yet there might be something in it.

Mrs. Adams saw another side to the question. "But, my lord, if we may suppose that such a great man might find himself sufficiently occupied with office in this continent, what must we think would be the case with his lady? What must a minister's wife, accustomed to the life of London and the English countryside, find here to reconcile her to what she loses?"

Lord Hemynge had a seed to plant. "Much what a North

115

American lady translated to London must find, Mrs. Adams—
novelty and variety. There are doubtless some women who
would find such changes overpowering. But Lady Hester, a
woman of great capacity, would meet her surroundings with
energy and dignity. She did so, certainly, during the Earl's illness in his later ministry. She served at times almost as a secretary of state—not in Wesminster, but in the antechamber to
the great man's sickroom."

"She serves England, then, as well as she serves her husband!"
Abigail declared with a flush of pride.

"I cannot suppose that any Roman matron ever served Rome
better," Lord Hemynge said with firm seriousness.

These conclusions touched a concern that was very lively in
Abigail's heart. For once she did not need to summon courage
to voice it, for her candor seemed to be invited.

"I wonder," she said reflectively, "I wonder whether we might
be growing women of such capacity in North America."

Lord Hemynge bowed slightly toward her, smiling. "I am
certain, Mrs. Adams, that you are."

It did not seem to Abigail that his manner was that of the
flatterer, and she was pleased by his courteous tribute.

Then John Adams spoke up with almost his first show of good
humor. "Our society is modest in comparison with that of
European capitals and courts, my lord. Our women conduct
themselves accordingly."

In the great room of the mansion, after the dinner, Lord
Hemynge summoned Tompkins to join his guests. He proposed
that Tom lead in the performance of more music for Mrs.
Adams, while he and Mr. Adams should retire to the library
for the discussion of business. The lady graciously agreed to
the suggestion, which in fact struck her as somewhat comically
superfluous. It was a long ingrained habit of hers to give gentlemen easy opportunity to proceed to the discussion of business

116

ree of her presence. Very often, in her house, they did not
avail themselves of the opportunity, and she was the auditor,
the observer, the witness to many an intense or grave or lively
debate around her table, or beside her hearth, on the great
issues facing the province and the Empire. On those rare occasions when she found it impossible to contain her own question, comment, or conclusion, her utterances were received with
respect rather than with special indulgence. Oh, her husband
had once or twice chaffed his sagacious Portia when her outburst had been from an especially deep conviction and voiced
with unusual spirit or heat. But he had never found it necessary
to correct her opinion on the score of justice, nor to chide her
for unbecoming assertiveness. Indeed, she knew that he valued
her opinion, and she knew that she was far more fortunate in
this respect than most wives in her acquaintance.

Lord Hemynge, by his beautifully polite deference to her
throughout the lavish dinner, had earned an hour alone with
John, she felt. Her dear husband had been unusually silent,
and she was confident that an occasion was being offered for
the expression of his ever enlightening and inspiring judgment
of business. She was glad that this elegant and accomplished
peer of the realm would learn something of John Adams' capacity for close thought in intimate discussion of affairs, to sup-
plement the heroic impression made by his display of powers
in the courtroom.

Oh, yes, Mrs. Adams felt, this was an happy occasion! The
glimpse Lord Hemynge had afforded of the heavy responsibilities borne by such a wife as the Countess of Chatham had
subtly inspired her with a superb confidence that she, too, knew
what it was to be the wife of a great man—that she, too, accepted as an honor the necessity to nurse any infirmity that
might touch her husband's body; and that she, too, might rise,
if required to do so, to convey the workings of his mind to his
fellow countrymen. As she saw her husband, moving rather
stiffly, precede Lord Hemynge into the library, she felt an overpowering love and gratitude for John Adams.

He has named me his Portia! she thought with a sense of triumph.

She turned to Tompkins with the best will in the world. The grotesqueness of his appearance, the exaggeration of politeness in his manner that amounted almost to servility, were nothing but pleasing to her. And as a woman, too, she was subject to an appeal in this waif's person that was lightly overlooked by such generous patrons as the Earl of Hemynge and Mr. Andrew Dubourg. It was his extreme thinness, the nervous emaciation of his countenance that drew her most nearly.

"Oh, Mr. Tompkins," she urged him with an eager warmth, "please make me acquainted with some of those tunes you have brought from London! That is"—she hesitated—"if you've had your supper."

❧

Lord Hemynge was not in the least uncomfortable, facing Mr. Adams in the privacy of the noble library of the Province House. He spoke easily and confidently of the new attitude to colonial policy that had been developed by Lord North's ministry. He observed that Mr. Adams was interested in spite of some inner discomfiture, some curious distaste for the circumstances of this conversation, a distaste that showed mainly in the grimness of his facial expression.

The colonial lawyer had accepted a glass of his lordship's Madeira, and sipped it occasionally as though its miraculous sun-baked mellowness masked a poison. He had accepted a tobacco pipe, and puffed it now and then with an air of censuring the ripe, tangy sweetness of the smoke he drew from it. As he listened to Lord Hemynge's account of the high intent of the ministry, he for long moments let his eyes focus on the peer's face in a scrutiny that a less assured speaker than his host might have felt was a forbidding, a thoroughly discomfiting stare.

But all of this was noted by the Earl with a certain respect

118

that was allied to his frank curiosity as to what the manners in intimacy were like of a provincial person of so great abilities as he knew Mr. Adams to be. The Earl of Hemynge recognized that the position of the first men to sit in the House of Lords as North American peers would be difficult. His own opinion was that for the health of the policy, these first representatives of the colonies should be persons of a conspicuous force of character. There would be many in the Parliament who would sneer at them, treat them as rustic provincials, and seek to overawe them. The veins of stubborn caution and skepticism, and even, he suspected, of belligerency, that he detected in Mr. Adams' bearing, were the very armor to protect him in the transformation that would be visited upon his fortunes.

After he had set forth the "mood" of the government, without revealing yet the honor that was to be a sequel to the government's action in that mood, Lord Hemynge felt that it was time for Mr. Adams to offer a comment. He invited it simply by waiting for it. He could sit through a long silence himself. If Mr. Adams could do so too, the peer was willing to let the colonial lawyer break it when he was ready to. But he did confess to himself, during this extraordinarily protracted wait, that he would be more comfortable, after all, when Mr. Adams broke his scrutiny of the Humbird face as well as his silence.

The truth is that the peer had observed his guest well. John Adams was experiencing an acutely painful siege of mixed emotions. Certainly he was imposing upon his faculties rigid controls of caution and skepticism, and he was nursing a secret antagonism, even hostility, toward his host. Where his wife's prejudice against the supposed manner, the rumored deportment, the imagined costume of a great nobleman of London had been rather swiftly dispelled by her current encounter with the reality of these things in the person of Edward Humbird, John Adams' own Bostonian antipathy was not subject to so pleasant a modification. When Lord Hemynge had waited

119

upon him in the modest house in Brattle Square, even though he had been feeling particularly unwell and fatigued, he had accepted the politeness and the adroit flattery of the peer as tolerable, and had been ready to grant, within limits, that the envoy appeared to be something in the way of a man of sense and capacity. But now, as guest in the nobleman's normal setting of luxury and elegance, he was struck all too forcibly by the creature's dandyism—saw in him some trace of the excesses of a Restoration fop, a beau, a flutterer. His dislike for the kind, and for its exemplar before him, moved perilously close to contempt.

It further galled John Adams that this fancy and absurd personage should be entrusted with important authority by the ministry, and even that he managed to speak of business with counterfeits in his bearing of learning, earnestness, and dignity. What a waste of opportunity that this plumaged fellow should have enjoyed the acquaintance of William Pitt, and should have conversed with him on Empire policy! that he should have had access to the formidable William Murray, Lord Chief Justice Mansfield, and should have dared to debate a point of law with him! A Bostonian almost had to come round to a grudging respect for the silk-swathed intruder if one must credit the allegation that he had commanded a ship for the Admiralty, and in it had visited the ancient ports of the Mediterranean and the Baltic.

And yet—and yet—it is not impossible that John Adams, in some most private recess of his mind or heart, was to a degree himself fluttered by the marked affability of this person who was, after all, an *English lord*, all belted and powdered, and the bearer of a coronet.

Yes. But how much of a man was he? Unfortunately even here it must be admitted that he was man enough to speak up handsomely for the policy of conciliation that was said to be developing in the Tory ministry of Lord North.

A fog of emotion and prejudice that would confuse and blind other men was not sufficient to extinguish John Adams' intel-

lectual lights. He heard and recognized what might be esti-
mated to be valid in the speech even of such a beau as his
present host, the Earl of Hemynge, envoy extraordinary from
His Majesty's Government to His Majesty's colonies in North
America. He offered his comment at last.

"My lord, this is an account of the intent of King, Lords,
and Commons such as I have never been privileged to hear
before. It would appear to incite far stronger hope for an early
reconciliation of our provincial governments with the British
Government than any of us here have supposed possible, in
this bloody and alarming year. If it is truly the intent of the
ministers to remove the causes of our persisting quarrels with
the administration, I believe that the resultant peace would be
welcome here with even greater rejoicing than would be the
case in England. But our experience has been consistent—our
pleas rebuffed, our communications ignored, our grievances
dismissed and further compounded. Is it possible, sir, that the
ministry is able to conceive the extent to which our confidence
in the justice of British government has been shaken? Are there
any radical measures a-drawing to relieve us of the alerted
suspicion that has spread abroad among us, as it properly must
among any people who persistently suffer injustice? The damage that has been done by injustice in the past ten years is
severe, my lord. Is the Prime Minister prepared to take the
real trouble that must be incurred to convince us that his intent is genuine, to repair that damage?"

In the course of his statement, John Adams' mind had risen
above his too ready distaste for the apparent character of the
man with whom he was closeted, to "the burning concerns of
his country."

Lord Hemynge felt the value of American honesty in the response he had drawn. "Your observations and your questionings
do you honor, Mr. Adams. Certainly we must have large
measures of magnanimity in the leading negotiators for the
ministry, and in the leading representatives of the colonies, if
we are to reach a resolution of the present discords."

121

"Magnanimity has been a quality missing in the councils of British government for ten years, my lord," Mr. Adams declared. "We in Massachusetts Bay have felt keenly the lack of it in the administrations that have succeeded Mr. Pitt's great ministry, and we have been driven to respond in kind. Some of the reasoning we have advanced in protest may have seemed fallacious in the councils at Westminster—but it has been submitted in an honest attempt to set forth the injuries of which our people are too sharply conscious."

Lord Hemynge was encouraged by his guest's expressions. He had a feeling of satisfaction that he had chosen well; that he was unmistakably on the "right track"; that Johnny Adams was indeed the "only hope." He was ready to make a further investment in candor.

"May I submit a thought for your consideration, Mr. Adams, which I believe may not have lodged in many minds in the Massachusetts Bay, especially in the Boston seat, in late years? It relates to the *causes* of the injustice you speak of. I suggest that the true causes of these acts have been ignorance, misinformation, misunderstanding, and on some occasions a culpable levity on the part of ministers with respect to colonial affairs, rather than any deliberate malice or intent to oppress. As an instance, I may assure you that the late Mr. Grenville experienced true amazement when he learned of the colonial resistance to his proposed Stamp Duty. As the protests gathered force, he was able to perceive in them only defiance, which indeed they exhibited plainly enough. It became impossible for him to conceive that his measures, so carefully drawn to replenish the imperial exchequer that was sadly depleted as a result of the French wars, might genuinely be considered injurious to the American provinces. Even Mr. Pitt, as he then was, did not oppose the Stamp Duty with any force until he had had time to heed the nature of the protests arriving from America. Mr. Townshend, I acknowledge, displayed levity in designating his paper, sugar, tea, and molasses taxes as 'external,' rather than as the 'internal duties' which your provincial legislature had declared were beyond the power of Parliament to impose. The levity in Townshend's motives was censurable—but many sober men in Parliament accepted his proposals as a proper acknowledgment of the colonial declarations of principle."

The envoy paused, to note that his guest still had the air of the provincial man hearing "an account of the intent of King, Lords, and Commons such as he had never heard before."

"The present administration has reached the conclusion that the causes of such misunderstanding must be corrected. We know that this conclusion is reached tardily. We refuse to admit that it has been reached 'too late.' We have examined all possible means of correcting the condition that compels the Parliament to legislate blindly for the American colonies. The one means we can discover of eradicating the prevailing ignorance, and the spread of misinformation about the colonial interest, is to introduce into the Parliament itself representatives of the North American colonies."

Again his lordship paused. He was conscious that Mr. Adams' stare had taken on again some of the frosty and forbidding quality that had receded from his aspect when he offered his first observation. Lord Hemynge's heart was in his business now.

"In effecting the introduction of North American representatives into the British Parliament, Mr. Adams, we must have the aid of colonial patriots. The breed is known in England as stout, as above intimidation. We intentionally circumvent the official channel that up to the present time has been our exclusive means of communication. We do *not* rely on the royal governors, nor on the customs commissioners, nor on any other Crown officials for advice in effecting the measure—I may go so far as to call it this measure of parliamentary reform. This is an action that may be known in future generations as the 'Glorious Revolution of 1770,' or possibly even more splendidly and justly as the 'North American Revolution'—just as actions resulting from the great Whig compact of 1688 are to this day known as the 'Bill of Rights Revolution.' "

Lord Hemynge felt that he had chosen his words fortunately. He had spoken of such great things as only England, relying upon her millions of true-born Englishmen, could accomplish. And indeed, the direction of John Adams' gaze had altered. He was no longer staring at the peer of the realm who was casting upon him a spell of historical fascinations. He had raised his eyes to gaze upon some remote object far above Edward Humbird's head, far beyond the dim paneled walls and richly laden bookshelves of this luxurious library in the Province House of Massachusetts Bay.

There was something in the man's silence that the sixth Earl of Hemynge found worthy of respect. Yet he must disturb him, seek to recall him to the present negotiation, secure again his undivided, if critical, attention.

"Is it not proper, Mr. Adams," he pressed his quarry gently, "that we should come first to Massachusetts Bay with news of this proposal? And for the colonial help we need?"

John Adams kept his host waiting for what was scarcely more than a murmured answer: "Yes, my lord—it is eminently proper." So much he could find ready to his tongue. But the tumult of his thoughts at this moment was too great to permit fuller speaking out on the great proposal.

For it was an irony, John Adams perceived, that the proposal *was* great; and that it had come from a government formed by the Tory Minister known to Englishmen everywhere as the warmest of the King's Friends. But suppose that it had come from William Pitt, ten years ago, when Boston, New York, Philadelphia, Charleston, like London herself, were flush with the victory over the Bourbon and proud with the highest sense they had ever contained of Great Britain's greatness. Suppose that later there had been colonial advocates in the Mother of Parliaments to support the voices of William Pitt and Edmund Burke in opposition to the oppressive

124

measures proposed in ignorance and levity. Or suppose that the proposal had come to Massachusetts Bay while James Otis' magnificent rallying cry of "No taxation without representation!" was fresh and persuasive. Suppose that it had come before Sam Adams had decided, for publication, that representation in Parliament was "impracticable"; and, in private, for purposes of keeping his Boston caucus under control, that representation at Westminster would thwart all hope of denying the claims of the Parliament to legislative authority over the colonies.

Mr. Adams could not estimate whether he had been sought out to give his counsel, or for some more onerous obligation in the negotiations that presumably were to be forthcoming. He had a sudden enlightenment as to the "capacity" of the nobleman whom he had taken for a beau or a fop. He recognized that Edward Humbird of Hemynge had submitted his program with great effect. The recognition made him wary.

"What are the terms of the proposed measure, or measures, which would bring about the inclusion of North American colonial representation in the Parliament, my lord?" he asked.

"The British subjects in North America will find that the terms are generous, Mr. Adams. They project that there shall be immediate elevations of six North American persons to peerages, so that they shall be seated in the House of Lords. It is stipulated that they shall be persons who have never held any office in the appointive power of the Crown. The American peers shall serve as an advisory council in the devising of a comprehensive system of American boroughs, so that as early as possible the colonies may be represented in the Commons."

The envoy paused, as though to give the eloquent colonial lawyer an opportunity to acknowledge the import of the information now disclosed to him. But John Adams' silence had again become so deep that Lord Hemynge felt that he must complete his revelation.

"Mr. Adams," he went on, "it is my very great privilege to inform you that in carrying out the mission entrusted to me by the ministry, I shall submit your name as the first among those of the colonial subjects who will be elevated to the American peerage I have mentioned. The elevation will be to the rank of Earl, the title will be hereditary, grants of money and land will be in the settlement. You may adopt such styling as pleases you—something on the lines of 'Earl of Braintree,' perhaps."

Again he gave Mr. Adams a chance to speak. Again the lawyer was strangely silent. Was it agitation, or sheer wonder, that had raised the flush to his countenance, giving his staring eyes somehow an appearance of the febrile? Lord Hemynge could understand that in one accustomed to the barren life of this remote province, the sudden prospect of elevation to such high place in the hierarchy of Empire must induce a momentary consternation.

He introduced a soothing note into his voice as he proceeded. "Mr. Adams, I judge that you may wish to enjoy a moment of solitary reflection upon this honor, which no doubt finds you unprepared and subject to something of surprise." His lordship made an easy gesture toward some papers spread upon a table, where the light from a cluster of candles illuminated them. "I invite, in fact I request you to read the despatches I have set out here for your attention. Certain correspondence of the Prime Minister—an opinion written by Lord Mansfield —a concurring declaration of support for the policy, written by Mr. Burke for the Marquis of Rockingham. May I leave you with these papers?"

Mr. Adams, who seemed to be drawing and expelling his breath with a certain labored difficulty, as though overcome by emotion, was unable to speak. He gave a hasty nod.

Lord Hemynge rose and moved toward the door. "You are welcome to examine those documents at your leisure. I shall join Mrs. Adams in the next room. If you wish to see me, to query any point raised in these despatches, I am at your disposal close at hand."

He waited at the door a moment for any word that his honored guest might wish to utter. Apparently there was none.

Lord Hemynge smiled, bowed impressively, then went out of the room, closing the door behind him.

Left alone, and with the offer of a peerage lingering in his ears, John Adams became something other than the man of sense his family, friends, neighbors, clients, and constituents knew him to be. After Lord Hemynge had closed the library door firmly behind him, Mr. Adams found his voice, and with a hoarseness that would have terrified Abigail, cried out: "No! Stop—wait!"

Conscious suddenly that he was deserted, he got up hastily from his chair, strode toward the door. His intent was to fling that door open with a force that would crash it against the wall at the far extremity of its swing, to give pursuit through the chambers of this detestable mansion till he cornered its present occupant, to seize that mockingbird peer by the collar, and to shake him until he had completely unspoken his late set of sneering speeches.

But the very force of his desire to inflict physical violence on his detested adversary was what saved him. His emotion was near suffocating him; it brought him so close to the point of collapse that he suddenly recognized its nature. It was his old enemy, furious anger, out of control.

He was driven to utter a sound, a moan, from the heart and the throat, as the gigantic effort he made to check the force of his fury began to take effect. He stretched out his arm, touched the firm wood of the doorway arch to support himself. The breaking of his progress caused him to stagger. He turned, and looked back over the short distance to the chair he had left a moment before. He saw that he must get back to it. The steps he took to reach it were unstable. He clung to the arm and back of the chair briefly before he could find the way to seat himself safely in it.

Then he sat there, alone, fighting himself, fighting his own bitter choler, fighting the very air of the room for sufficient breath. He sat there a full quarter of an hour before he knew himself the reasonable man again. But if reasonable, it was with a difference. He was spent, wasted, outraged, and ill.

The thought of his wife came to him: Abigail, faithful, innocent, fortifying—his friend beyond compare.

"We must get out of this house, she and I. We must make our escape as soon as possible."

But they were, he felt, in a public place, bound, chained by rules of conduct that they must observe. And he still could not trust himself to move, not in this exhausted condition. He leaned his head against the cushioned back of the chair he sat in. He closed his eyes, rested, waiting with a new-found patience for a more complete return of his strength.

Presently he opened his eyes, and was oppressed by the silence, the stillness of the air, the very steadiness of the glow of the candlelight. He would have been grateful for fresh gusts of air, even from a North Atlantic tempest, to make that steady yellow light flicker and gutter.

Then his glance fell upon those papers spread for him, as though they were a banquet, by the satanic peer of the realm who had trapped him here.

He recalled the substance they were supposed to confirm. Slowly now, not trusting himself to expend any appreciable energy in the motion, he rose from the chair and walked to the table. His eye fell first on the letter written by Mr. Burke. He looked away from that, and saw the signature, *William Murray, Baron Mansfield, Lord Chief Justice,* affixed to another sheet.

John Adams' struggle to regain his composure had ended in success. The intense curiosity he must normally feel to inspect a document from the hand of Great Britain's first man-of-law— his own contemporary across the sea, his compatriot, the head of his own profession—was now awakened in him. He lifted it from the table, held it under the light for the best advantage of his eyesight, and began to read. His professional nature came to full awareness of the fascinating dualism of Mans-

128

field's intellect. "For . . . and Against . . ." What balance would he find in the ancient canon of English law for the impudent assault directed only now upon the defenses of America's integrity, decency, and love of liberty? Of course! The Scottish peers . . . the Act of Union, of 1707 . . .

John Adams was himself again. Closeted in a library, he was reading, with avidity, a manuscript containing a dissertation upon great issues of the law, and upon the burning concerns of his—and Lord Mansfield's—country.

To sit and listen, without singing, to music that was not meant to be sung, was a new experience for Mrs. Adams. When Tompkins announced to her that he and his fellow musicians would perform for her the Concerto in B-flat, a work of Mr. Handel's that was a special favorite of Lord Hemynge, she felt that she would like to be free to move among the players, to look at the notes they were reading, and to study "how they did it." But Tompkins clearly expected her to remain in her seat near the hearth, and she did so with a slight sense of being left uncomfortably alone. But then they began to play, and she forgot herself entirely.

The concerto was written in four parts—slow, fast, slow, and fast. The first of the plaintive, the wistful notes from Tompkins' pipe—a very fine French hautboy—prompted Abigail to breathe a soft whisper to herself: "Shepherds!" And as they did in classic pastoral verses, so now in the ordered measures of another art, the shepherds tended their flocks, with ample leisure for inviting the muses, for engaging in formally tender passages with the delectable shepherdesses, for moving in the patterns of a stately dance, for reflection, for calm, for a perfection of exquisite happiness. . . .

But the life and art that had inspired the contriving of these sounds were far remote from Boston and Braintree. The colonial lawyer's wife, the country parson's daughter dreamed for a moment of what remained in the Great World, of Attica and Sicily, of Rome and Tuscany—she omitted the formal but perhaps tainted chivalry of France—and of the green-shaded parks of Tudor England, where velvet lawns had been as unflawed carpets for the satin-shod feet of the Great Queen, Elizabeth—Oriana.

She shook her head gently to cast off vain reveries, and looked up to find that Tompkins had crossed the room to her. There was a hopeful complacency in his expression that Mrs. Adams again found quite irresistible.

"Yes, Mr. Tompkins—that is most agreeable." She smiled. "And so very well performed!"

In Tompkins' view, she was no more than just. The hautboy concerto was *his* masterpiece if not Mr. Handel's, and he had rehearsed it so painstakingly late into the previous night that his patron had sent him packing off toward the cupola to pipe it beyond closed doors at the top of the house.

❦

When Lord Hemynge returned to the great room of the house from the library, leaving Mr. Adams closeted with a set of interesting despatches, he found his faithful secretary on a low hassock at the lady's feet, talking a spate of words about music in London to her. The Bostonian amateurs were reading *pianissimo* a sonata for violin and figured bass. His lordship surveyed the scene with a pleasure that was partly derived from the sense that the opening of his negotiation with Mr. Adams had gone very well. He stood for a moment listening to the performers. They reached a double bar, and paused. The peer walked to them, and with a quiet thanks dismissed them.

Tompkins became conscious of what was happening, rose and bowed his excuses to Mrs. Adams with a touch of the confidential in his manner. Then he went quickly to guide the other two musicians from the house, and to perform a steward's duty in conferring upon them his lordship's reward.

130

Mrs. Adams had hoped to see her husband and their host return together from the library, their discussion of business completed, and with the evidences of affability between them somewhat more mutual than had been the case earlier. But she accepted without concern the fact that Lord Hemynge reappeared alone. She never challenged the comings and goings of men when they were engaged in business. And now his lordship chose to take a standing position not far from her at the hearth, resting an arm easily on the mantel.

"I must hope, ma'am, that the music has been agreeable to you?" he inquired.

"It has been, my lord," Abigail replied. "And Mr. Tompkins has afforded some information about London customs and tastes in music that has been instructive."

"I have discovered, Mrs. Adams, that the study of music is of all studies the most edifying. It affords not only instruction, but it gives pleasure, as well. I have a curious fancy that one of the greatest boons England could confer upon these remote North American provinces would be a great increase in the export of music from our island to your continent." His lordship added an afterthought: "To be perpetually free of internal or external duty of any kind, of course."

He maintained a sober countenance, but Mrs. Adams smiled.

"This export, my lord, might be one commodity for which our countrymen here would willingly pay a duty." Then she, too, had an afterthought. "That is, within reason."

The peer moved quickly from his place at the hearth to a chair closer to his lovely guest, and sat facing her with an appearance of thoroughly engaged attention.

"My dear lady, this is the time when our causes must be mended," he began with great earnestness. "You are aware that I am here, entrusted with a mission whose end is to reconcile the interest of England with that of her colonies on this coast. This journey to Boston has been for me a voyage of discovery. The town, I find, is English; and the province, too, must be so. But we of London do not know you with any justice or exactitude, and you have been put off in your understanding of England by errors and misrepresentations. The time has come when New England must be brought into the orbit of England's power and cultivation. The deprivation we have just spoken of—this deprivation from the edification of the music we know in London—is only one of many which must be ended. And England, in her turn, has been deprived of the services of men of such capacity, and such magnanimity, as Mr. Adams. The ministry is only now awakening to such lacks and errors and misunderstandings. My very great honor has been to disclose to your husband, only now, evidence that the British government of King, Lords, and Commons has moved to acknowledge the injustices suffered by the true-born Englishmen on this continent from careless infringement of their rights. And a measure is now offered to restore those rights and liberties, to repair what has been damaged, and to invite hope for a proper unity of interest in the future." He paused.

Abigail could perceive that he intended to disclose to her what he had disclosed to her husband. She felt suddenly that she had much rather hear Lord Hemynge's "evidence" from John Adams than from the noble emissary himself.

"The reassurance you promise will be needed by more men than my husband, sir," she reminded him.

"Indeed, I acknowledge that to be true, Mrs. Adams," Lord Hemynge said. "And to convey such intelligence, we must have the advices of such a man of genius as Mr. Adams. The measure that the government is prepared to effect is this: It is to offer representation in the Parliament to the North American colonies—to the Massachusetts Bay first of all."

Abigail Adams felt a suffocating agitation in her breast. She turned a little pale. So it was with business on this scale of vast importance that John must be wrestling, alone in that library. It was veritably what he had called a "statequake." The conspiracy to keep him engaged in public business had extended even to London, now. Abigail pressed her right hand against her heart, turned her gaze to the glowing fire on the hearth.

Her host recognized that she must be moved. When he spoke again it was more gently. "I do not see how any government could offer more hopeful reassurance, more certain proof, to the people of a troubled province," he suggested, inviting her concurrence.

But she could not speak yet. These were news that must reach her in the terms in which only John Adams could set them forth. And she felt, too, that this was no time for him to be left alone.

Lord Hemynge went on. "The people of the Massachusetts, and to some extent of the other colonies, have nurtured a sense of aloofness from England. It has been more divisive than the remoteness which is a physical fact in the condition of the colonies. England today summons Massachusetts Bay and her sister colonies to take part in government of the British Empire, from the heart of that Empire, at Westminster. Your men of intellect and capacity shall enter the councils of high policy and government. There shall be properly among them, men of rank, station, noble title. The ladies of the great houses of Massachusetts Bay, New York, Virginia, Carolina, shall meet the ladies of the great houses of London—of Surrey and Kent, Devon and Essex. They should have done so long ago."

The touch of a shrinking kind of emotion which could now be seen in Mrs. Adams' aspect enhanced her beauty in Lord Hemynge's eyes. "It is time, Mrs. Adams," he said with forceful distinctness, "that such a lady as yourself had the authority to set the fashions in Boston, and to exercise in the brilliant assemblages that gather in larger capitals, the manners that grace yourself so nobly."

Abigail's agitation was intensified, as though she had been affronted. Of the many emotions at war within her, it seemed to her possible to identify two as of a highly unwelcome character: they were cold alarm and warm indignation, an ill mixture. But somewhat to her own surprise she found breath to speak, and to hold her voice upon an even tone.

"I cannot suppose that anyone save yourself, Lord Hemynge, has ever spoken to a housewife of Boston in this sort. We are aware, sir, that Massachusetts Bay is *not* one of the great kingdoms of the world. We have received this country from our fathers, who cultivated its lands with their own hands, and so do we today. We can do no other than to love our country as it is, and as it may become with the fruits of our labors. Boston, I fear, has no burning ambition to send her sons to London—no more than to any other of the 'great capitals' of the world, from which we have lived, as you say, my lord, 'remote and aloof.'" She was looking directly at her host now. "These are questions with which my husband and his friends must deal, sir. He is fit to answer you as I am not."

The Earl of Hemynge was convinced that this demonstration of modesty was honest, that it concealed no eagerness for elevation. "I have only now submitted the proposal of the ministry to your husband, ma'am, in all explicitness," he assured her. He smiled, and went on. "Mr. Adams is first among gentlemen of the North American colonies to be sought for a seat in the House of Lords. He shall represent this province, the Massachusetts Bay, as an earl among the peers of the Empire. You shall be his countess. We have urgent need of such as his soon-to-be-lordship, and your present ladyship, in both London and Boston." He bowed, smiling.

What she was hearing was unbelievable—yet even so it did not have the mean sound of a gigantic mockery. But something must be said to fend it off.

"I am not anybody's ladyship, sir," she protested. She might have added that it was impossible for her to think of her husband as anybody's lordship. But lordship or no lordship, and God forbid that there should be any, what she wanted now was to find her husband, cling to him, ask him the truth, and hear his judgment exercised upon these fantasies. Like John Adams an hour earlier, she was constrained by the sense that they

134

were in a public place, and were bound by rules—chains—of conduct that forbade her to run and seek the man she loved, in the waste spaces of this gilded house.

She sought within herself a further response that would free her from confrontation by Lord Hemynge's smiling, complacent, expectant attitude.

"I am sure, my lord," she began—"I am sure that my husband deserves more honor than he ever gets, and I am sure you speak considerately of this honor. . . ." She stopped, because she could not bring herself to feel that it was an honor.

Then there was the sound of a door opening. John Adams stood in the entrance to the library, a soft light behind him, the bright illumination of the larger room he now faced seeming to strike him momentarily with a kind of blindness of shock.

Abigail Adams was stricken at sight of him with a renewed alarm. Never had John Adams worn an aspect more grim, more severe. Abigail, his wife, saw that he was drained of all energy, all health. Never before had she seen him in such a state of exhaustion.

Now he moved toward them at the hearth. His wife watched his steps with astonishment that they were so steady. Still some distance from them, he stopped his advance.

"I have read the despatches you left with me, sir," he said. Perhaps he would have gone on but that Abigail, with a little murmur, rushed to support him. She took his arm, pressed herself against his side.

"John, you are not well," she said quickly. She could see now that he had been through a fit of anger since he had been out of sight in this house. Had there been a dispute with Lord Hemynge? No, impossible. The peer could not conceivably have undertaken to speak so ingratiatingly to her if there had been an hostile passage between her husband and himself while they were closeted in the library.

The Earl of Hemynge spoke confidently, invitingly. "Then, Mr. Adams, perhaps you are ready to charge me with the answer I shall return to His Majesty and his First Minister, Lord North?"

135

Holding fast to John Adams' arm, Abigail felt a tension spread its grip over his frame.

"Yes, certainly, my lord. I must give you an answer for His Majesty and Lord North." The hoarseness in his voice, the flush in his face, sent a dash of terror to Abigail's heart.

"John, you are not well!" she cried. "I beg that you will not speak nor think of this great matter any further tonight." She turned with a commanding urgency to Lord Hemynge. "I am sorry, my lord—I implore your pardon. But my husband is in a state of too great fatigue. He must not enter upon discussion of so grave a concern at this moment. Is it possible you will be so kind, so good, as to spare him further business this evening? May he not send you an answer tomorrow—wait on you where you will?"

Lord Hemynge felt the force of her appeal, and indeed found that he shared some of her anxiety with respect to Mr. Adams. "But certainly, Mrs. Adams," he said. "If Mr. Adams has suffered a seizure—"

"Oh, thank you, my lord." She turned back to her husband. "John—please say nothing now. We must return to our house as quickly as possible. Do not think any further of this business. You are not in fit condition to touch it."

Observing with some surprise that John Adams was permitting her to have her way, she turned again to Lord Hemynge.

The peer immediately spoke up again. "If it is advisable that Mr. Adams retire for immediate rest, I shall be glad to place a chamber in this house at your disposal," he offered.

"No, my lord, thank you," Mrs. Adams replied. "Will you only assist us to return to our dwelling?"

"I shall order the conveyance at once." Lord Hemynge turned and walked from the room.

Mrs. Adams guided her husband to a chair, and knelt beside it.

"What is this conduct, Abigail?" John Adams demanded, still with the heavy hoarseness in his throat. "Why have you interrupted me, put us off clearing up this insane business?"

"You must pardon my presumption, John, my dearest. I can

136

see that you are truly not fit to conduct business tonight. Do not hold it against me that I have asked for time. What I have done is best, I am certain of it. Only trust me tonight, John. That is all I ask."

Actually, she trembled to face what she had done. No woman had ever before been so forward as she, to intervene between the King's Messenger and the object of his message. But that she was having her way gave her a sense of confidence that she was right, and was known to be so by either or both of the men between whom she had come.

John Adams sat sunk in a dark mood in his chair, Abigail remaining beside him. Presently Lord Hemynge returned to the room with word that the servant had brought around Mr. Adams' chaise. His guests rose, Mrs. Adams holding close to her husband's arm as they moved to the hall.

Lord Hemynge held her mantle for her. The servant helped John Adams into his greatcoat. Abigail, noting the dark and inexpressive condition of her husband's features, was confirmed in her now lively sense that it was entirely proper that he should take leave of the government's emissary in this way. So grave a question as had been submitted should gravely be considered overnight.

"Perhaps it will be acceptable that I wait upon Mr. and Mrs. Adams at their dwelling in Brattle Square tomorrow—at noon?" Lord Hemynge proposed.

John Adams caught his wife's expression of approval. He spoke stiffly. "That will be acceptable, my lord. I am sorry to have interrupted our conversation."

"Thank you for the musical entertainment, my lord," Mrs. Adams murmured.

In a moment they were free of the house which had held them too long in holding them at all. When they were settled in the chaise, they were made sharply aware of the extreme chill in the night air. But this air seemed pure and healthy to them, because it was so different from the warm, bright, candle-lit air of the house in which they had been offered an earldom.

137

8

HOME AGAIN, MRS. ADAMS URGED HER HUSBAND TO RETIRE TO bed at once for the rest that was surely his greatest need. He ignored the suggestion, led the way to the hearthside, stirred up the banked embers of the fire. Then he shifted a chair and sat down in it close to the blaze, watching the fire as though its increase were the object of an intense curiosity or anxiety to him.

Abigail quietly busied herself in filling a small copper kettle with water, bringing out her priceless canister of tea leaves, setting a tray with a tea service, and adding to it some biscuits. She put the kettle on the hob over the blaze, placed the tray on the low seat of the settle, and brought up a stool which she put close to her husband's chair. She sat down beside him, waiting for the water to boil, and for their thoughts to come to the point of utterance.

The extent and seriousness of his fatigue and his infirmities were impressed upon John Adams' consciousness by the events of this climactic night more forcibly than by any other occasion that had yet confronted him. The pains in his chest that had disturbed him much too often in the past year; the flagging of his energy; the maddening depletion of his physical strength; the more frequent outbursts of anger; the heavy foreboding he could not entirely stave off as to the effect on his family's safety and comfort that must follow from his own actions, those actions that had grown out of his deepest conviction as to what was right and *must* be done—all of these in turn, or sometimes in companies, or treading upon one another's heels, had haunted him. At times they had seemed to touch his heartbeat, giving it an unfamiliar and alarming incertitude in far too many watchful and troubling hours through the long year 1770.

What a year to come to Boston—what a doomed and fatal year! And all of its ills, all these slings and arrows of outrageous fortune had been shot almost at random, in carelessness, in despicable levity, or in a perverse stupidity from Old England to New. Even more particularly, they had been directed from London to Boston, from St. Stephen's Chapel to the State House—from the sick and corrupted Mother of Parliaments to the reluctantly, the desperately and, in the end, the honorably resistant General Court. Men born to them, men who revered them *must* speak out and stand firm for English liberties, if need be against England herself!

Here were elements, in truth, of tragedy: a tragedy of errors. Only, it was impossible now, for all the small and mean diversions, to undergo the purgation by all the pity and the shame of it—to feel the fury that should be called forth by the fatal spell of this spectacle of folly. For it could not cease to cast a spell, nor to be of the first importance, this struggle—not while England was England, not while English law still held its balance, not while Chatham still lived among Englishmen.

But it did, it did—it ceased to be magnificent when stupidly they set out earldoms, like spangled lures, exceeding at last their hundred other fumbles through a decade.

What had a *peerage* to do with that man who, in the night of March the fifth, had been quietly joined with a gathering of friends in the house of Mr. Henderson Inches at the south end of Boston, where the ringing of bells at nine o'clock was immediately supposed a signal of fire in the city?

What had it to do with that man, when he snatched up his

hat and cloak, and hurried abroad with his companions to do what could be done to quench the fire, or to help those of their friends who might be in danger from it?

What had it to do with that man when in the street, in that late winter night, he learned that British soldiers had fired on the people, near the Town House, killing some and wounding others?

Had that man earned a peerage by giving all of his immediate concern, on that occasion, to the safety of his wife and family, whom he had left in their modest little home facing upon the barracks and the drill ground?

He had a wife—and what a wife! He had a family—and what a family!

He had walked across Boston to give them such reassurance and protection as he might against the threat, the reality, of turmoil and catastrophe stirring abroad. He had reached in his walk the bloody ground in King Street, where a full company of soldiers had been summoned, to hold their guns aimed, at the ready. He had seen them, seen their kneeling position; he saw the blood in the snow, knew what the soldiers had done. And he had walked straight on, toward his family, by the only passage open to him, by the passage that forced him to walk in front of the cold and deadly mouths of those ready-aimed muskets, where a plain and a proud and a just man must pass unflinchingly, as John Adams did.

What had a peerage to do with an anxious man who had taken that walk, faced those arms amidst his outraged and incredulous fellow townsmen?

How could that man be elevated to the coronet who had, in the morning of March the sixth, received in his humble office the weeping and demoralized friend of the lost and bewildered soldier, who sought in despair a man of law to state his case before the bar of justice? The honest man of law had with misgiving and resentment scolded and stormed at the frightened fellow, the Irish Infant he was called, who was acting for the imprisoned Captain Preston. The lawyer warned the man to expect nothing—warned him that this cause was untouchable, save only on the basis that the truth must be submitted, the truth as it could be determined only by evidence. The soldier and his friend had displayed a certain pride and dignity then in their extremity—God help them, they asked only the right to submit their truth for a fair judgment under English law. For the young Captain had not put off the citizen when he put on the soldier. . . .

Pity, a human compassion, a sense of professional honor owing to English law by its advocates, had invested the honest man that morning. He had said: "On such terms I will undertake Captain Preston's cause. For no man should go without a defender before the law in the courts of the province of Massachusetts Bay."

John Adams had reached the conclusion in this cause that the soldier in Boston, wretched conservator of the peace that he might be, was nevertheless in fact the innocent agent of folly in the far-away Senate and Chamber of Council. The guilt lay elsewhere—higher, higher.

Now John Adams felt, in this December midnight, that the guilty had reached out to touch *him*, because he knew where the essential guilt lay. The guilty were seeking to raise *him* higher, higher, where he should be much closer to them, where his candor would be stopped by the cares of emolument. They, the guilty, even had the satanic penetration to know that their hook, with its lure, would be momentarily enticing, because it was baited with—Chatham!

These were injuries that wounded deeply; they were insults that fevered the honest man's brow; they were bribes that shamed the very belly of a Bostonian fit to call himself a man.

This was final. A man must face the authors of such insidious enticements and declare his independence from them. If the rulers of a great nation, an Empire—an edifice of state built clean and fresh only yesterday for a great family of peoples, by such a giant as Chatham—could fall to this level in trafficking and chaffering, then those among the tribes of that

141

nation, those among the provinces of that Empire that yet retained their virtue, likewise must declare their independence of it.

This was final. There was no turning back.

But what an ordeal this fatal necessity must impose upon a man's beloved wife, his cherished family! Perhaps the necessity was not yet fatal, not yet final, not quite yet completely a necessity?

This was in truth a man's extremity.

Pray God that it may not demand what it appears to demand.

Abigail Adams, seated close beside her husband, waited patiently for him to speak to her. She knew he was absorbed in a meditation, a troubled one, upon great and perhaps dire things. Oh, she could have spoken to him tonight. She might have invited the revelation from him gently and honorably. But again she preferred it to come from him, as it always had done. In the past, his communication to her of the great tidings was most often confident, rarely doubting, and not infrequently he broke to her even the grave or hateful or bewildering news with an assurance that was gallant. He was beyond compare—in courage, integrity, justice, strength, fidelity, spirit—in everything. She remembered how safe she had felt in his protection through the drawn-out hours that had dragged so heavily along the fatal night of March the fifth. She remembered how swift she had been to stanch her tears when he told her the next day of his decision to engage for the defense of the accused British soldiers, held in prison upon the Crown's charge of murder.

Abigail knew that even on those very rare occasions when she had opposed her husband—and she had done so only when his friends sought to engage him in the troubling public business of the town and the province, and it was clear that he could not resist their appeal, even though he responded to it reluctantly—she had never hindered him. At least, in humility, she prayed God that she had not done so; and, with equal

142

humility, she felt that she was entitled to believe that she had not.

But there was an end to everything, and Abigail recognized that she *had* hindered her husband tonight, in the great rooms of the Province House. She knew that in his agitation and his fatigue, he would have spoken out harshly and in anger a sharp rejection of the proposal that had been made to him in behalf of the British government by its envoy, the Earl of Hemynge. She had deliberately created a diversion to prevent his answer. She was too much concerned by her husband's state of exhaustion now to examine in her conscience the motive that had led her to make that diversion. She only knew that she had been irresistibly impelled to act as she had done, and she did not now feel that she had done ill.

As to the transactions of this astonishing evening, she might have agreed with the terms of Lord Chatham's prevision that they would be seen as monstrous. Yet in her own mind, she was not shocked by this monstrous thing—if it was monstrous. She was agitated by the prospect that had been opened so briefly before her, and which she knew her husband had contemplated for a longer and more searching hour. But a voice that would not be stilled, and that was not very small in her breast, persisted in asserting: "It is only just that such an honor should come to John Adams. Such elevation must be difficult to endure. Truly, to be sought out for it, is to be asked to sacrifice private happiness. My husband is entirely worthy of this honor, this demand—he is even capable of making this sacrifice."

Abigail had a healthy relish for the good things of life and the pleasures of society. But it was essentially true of her that she did not wish to be committed to a mode of living that called for constant adjustment to pomp and circumstance. She was bred to a certain mistrust of a customary luxury.

Still, several events recently had suggested to her mind that Boston, after all, was perhaps a dim and obscure, a very limited sphere for the exercise of John Adams' great powers. She herself could be content in this sphere, and happy to see her husband excelling all men in it. But if translation to a larger sphere were to be offered in good faith, she could give consideration to such an offer, independently of her husband's consideration, and she was capable of seeing its merits.

What was it Lord Hemynge had said, when she asked him what the Countess of Chatham would find in North American society? "Much what a North American lady translated to London must find—novelty and variety. She would meet her surroundings with energy and dignity!" Except that this moment in the firelight beside her husband was a solemn one, Mrs. Adams must have smiled.

Of course, she knew that Lord Hemynge's mission to Boston must fail. But she found it in her heart to hope that the failure need not be hurled in his pleasant face with the bruising force of an insult. After all, if he was not the finest man, he was certainly the most persuasive gentleman she had met in any company. Perhaps it was a little deep of her, but she knew that her husband and his stout Boston friends would be better off without knowledge of this, her secret opinion.

The water was boiling. With the comforting silence between husband and wife still unbroken, Abigail moved to the small tasks of brewing the tea, sprucing up the tray, filling the cups, handing one to John, serving herself.

After they had sipped the brew, she broke the spell that was upon them by asking, "Does it warm you clear through, John?"

Still gazing at the fire he murmured, "Yes. It is grateful."

Presently their cups were set down, and she was again simply sitting at his side. But even in his abstraction he could not fail to become sensible of the sweet expectancy of her attitude. She was waiting for him to speak to her.

And he did, taking her hand into his own.

"No man has ever had such a friend as this."

Yes, he used that word in his moments of deepest feeling,

144

and to hear him apply it to herself was a great joy. The emotion she felt on hearing it now invited a choking in her throat, and tears, but she controlled herself quickly.

"My dearest friend and I must remove quickly to Braintree," she said serenely, making it a declaration of great certainty. Nevertheless she was actually feeling uncertain, and it was with more of persuasion in her tone that she went on: "I think I have known that we must leave Boston for a long time, John. But now we have Joe Warren's advice. Of course he is right. He could not have spoken as he did if he were not serious. What he said in this room yesterday was said in spite of his desire to have you close at hand to help him and Mr. Adams in the public business here at Boston. But even so, he put it firmly that you should be better away from the plagues of public business, better with the cares of the farm on your hands. You shall have much rest and solitude, and if you wish, some quiet study, through the winter. In the spring, the planting and tending of the land will occupy you. It will be the saving of you, John—the saving of all of us."

Still John Adams said nothing.

She pressed him gently. "I know you must be in agreement with my thought, John. But tell me that this is so."

His voice when he answered was low and even, kept so by careful control. "Yes, it is so, Abigail. I have damaged my position in Boston fatally. This is a blow to me because it is hard upon my family. I find myself bearing such misfortunes ill. The impression I have of lowered health makes them no easier to bear. Yes, let us go to Braintree. Tending the farm will restore my forces, if they can be restored."

His wife's voice was broken by a sob as she said: "I must believe that our friends honor you and admire you only as you deserve, John. And as for Boston, after all you have done for this town, surely the people here cannot be so ungrateful . . ." She had to stop herself to catch a breath. "And if they should be so, it appears that London would receive you gladly." Her emotion surged so strong against her will that she failed to observe the stiffening, the restoration to fighting trim that this reference produced in him.

"Ha! London today has dropped beneath contempt," he said sharply. "The ministry has shown its hand at last. It cannot propose nor persuade, judge nor convince—it can only offer to buy."

Abigail, in the pain that had stricken her on hearing his quietly bitter statement of defeat, still missed the stirring change in him wrought by her reference to London. "Isn't it true, John," she asked in her weakness, "that the ministry has tried to honor you? Isn't there a kind of justice in this offer?"

"Yes!" he cried. A surge of the fury he had known an hour earlier shook him. He rose from his chair, moved abruptly to stand at the hearth, facing her, and a flush spread over his countenance. "Yes, there is a kind of justice in it: a cheapjack, pandering justice. You cannot have been deceived by it. I have defended an idiot officer and eight blundering troopers of His Majesty's forces against inconvenient charges in a colonial court. Who could have supposed the affair was of such importance that the reward for this pleading should turn out to be a peerage? What kind of a pack of knaves has our government fallen into? Who could ever have supposed such effrontery?"

Abigail had risen now, and she stood close to the chair her husband had left, letting her hand rest upon its back. She faced him fair and honestly, once again sure of her ground.

"I was afraid that you would speak exactly so to the Earl of Hemynge, John," she began her confession firmly. "That is why I made our apologies and sought our leave from the house in such haste."

He could not look at her as he asked accusingly: "You desired me to give a soft answer to this fawning courtier?"

"Not a soft answer"—she conceded so much to his mood—"though soft answers have been known to turn away wrath, and I think they may turn away bribes, too. I desire only that

146

you make an honest answer, John—and a proper one, with all the civility that you can muster." She knew that her husband could not have summoned the soft answer, which, in truth, was what she did desire him to make to Lord Hemynge. But she could not abandon the hope for something close to it, not without speaking a word in its defense to her angry man.

John Adams looked straight at her, his passion subsiding a little. "Civility? Propriety? To be served up in rejecting the most utterly base proposal that could have been offered to an American man of honor. Why? I do not understand."

"I am sure it is *my* understanding that is at fault, John," she said softly.

He scarcely heard her. "This is a monstrous mockery, Abigail. How can I address the man who mouths it to me, without heat? How can I conceal the disgust I feel?"

No, her understanding was not at fault, after all, Abigail realized. She understood perfectly that her husband despised the offer that had been made to him. And equally, her understanding told her that there was something decent, if mistaken, in Lord Hemynge's intention that should be corrected, since it must be, in terms other than those of "heat" and "disgust."

"Of course the proposal comes as something monstrous to you, John, just at this time, after your services in the trial," she submitted. "It appears that they judge you have made a bid for honors, and they are responding fifty-fold. It has the aspect of an over-rich reward, of a gigantic bribe. The ministry is made to look as though it has utterly forgotten that justice alone may be a sufficient motive in some men's minds for great effort, even for sacrifice. But John, if this proposal were made to various gentlemen of Virginia, Pennsylvania, or New York, who had not been through such tragic ordeals as our Boston men have known—do you think that to them it would appear so monstrous? If they were men of capacity, enjoying good reputation, might they not be forced to admit that to be approached with this proposal were reasonable? The end is one

147

that many such persons desire—the settlement of the issues between ourselves and the British government. If such men of capacity, in those other colonies, found the proposal to be one founded in error, why should they necessarily think it also monstrous, or corrupt? They might feel that it was sensible, even proper, though not agreeable to them. For many reasons they might refuse the honors offered. But would they find it necessary to do so with 'heat' or 'disgust'? Why should they?"

He was watching her face closely. She could see that she had moved him a little. He reflected a moment when she paused. Then he shook his head; the sense of angry revulsion was back upon him.

"'Error'?" He picked it out. "Error is much too kind a name for this—this shameless bribe. It stems from some kind of deep, smooth-faced duplicity. It is hateful to me that this business should have touched me."

Abigail was swift and clear. "It is only just and proper that when the British government undertakes to create high offices to be filled by American subjects of the Crown, the first such place should be offered to you. You have refused offers of place before, and I am sure you must always do so when you believe that acceptance would restrict your liberty of conscience and your honesty of thought and action. I am very glad and proud that you are like that, John."

She paused, inviting him to look at her. For she *was* proud, and she held her head high. He gave her no more than a dark glance.

She went on with her old familiar modesty. "I know that you have seen documents and secret despatches from the ministers of which I know nothing. But tell me, John, have they *proved* that the offer from His Majesty's government is *not* made in good faith? I must suppose that Lord Chatham is familiar with the proposal if only because the envoy uses his name so freely. Are we certain that this move may not be a true victory for the conciliation policy that William Pitt and Mr. Burke have supported so long? Must they not suppose, in London, that they do

148

genuine honor to you, and to whomsoever else may be concerned, in proposing that you be among the first to represent America in the Parliament?"

John Adams was listening to her with a reluctant interest. Abigail accepted his present scrutiny easily, and was ready for his question, or his challenge. When it came it was not soft— not soft at all.

"My wife is not advising me that I could accept this offer of a peerage, this 'Earldom of Braintree,' and retain any shred of honesty?"

She left her place, and went to him standing there at the hearthside, the "No" already on her tongue. She rested her hand lightly on his arm and repeated it many times: "No—no —no—no! No, John—never!"

Somehow she gave the simple negative the force of a glorious affirmation. John Adams' free hand found its way to hers, covered it where it rested so gently, scarcely perceptibly, on his forearm. But even so close to her, when he spoke his thoughts, he gazed away from her, down toward the weakening blaze.

"How rightly I should be despised if I were to take up such a proposed elevation, Abigail!" he said. "Sam Adams, Joe Warren, James Otis, even—they should all turn upon me violently. Or consider this: if such an offer should come to John Hancock, for example, and he should accept it. Why, I—" What would he do? He gave her time to wonder. "I should lead the Sons of Liberty in hanging him from the Tree—in effigy, I hope."

"And John," Abigail mildly added to these horrors, "you should put me aside from you if you believe for a moment that I could covet the title 'Countess of Braintree.'"

The sound of the female honorific forced his eyes open. It occurred to him for the first time that any woman, even his wife, might see some attraction in being lifted to the rank of countess. The thought gave him pause, but did not invite his indulgence. Abigail's assurance that she was not charmed by the prospect was all that mattered.

"It is as I thought, of course. You could not desire this for me or for yourself—nor for any honest person in Massachusetts Bay."

"No, I could not—never, for us in Massachusetts Bay." She had moved away from him now and faced him across the little distance that her place by the chair allowed them. "But when I think of the visitors we have had occasionally from New York and Pennsylvania and Virginia, it seems to me, John, that some persons among them, honest though they may be, might conceivably desire it. John, my dearest, I am glad that 'his lordship' came with this proposal first of all to *you*. Your rejection of it surely will set the matter straight. Your example defines the only true American position with respect to such honors."

John Adams' gaze could not leave his wife's face, so serious it was, and so warmly animated, as she spoke her honest mind. And she was bringing him around, away from the desperate sense of outrage and grief that had shaken him when, in his fatigue, he had become aware that the royal favor had reached out toward him with a strangling grasp. Abigail's beautiful exercise in reason, in application not of the Golden Rule, but of the Golden Mean, drew from him at last a smile.

"You are Portia, my lass!" he murmured with a certain wonder. "What you say is fair. Except that I hope to high heaven the fact that this *thing* has been offered to me may remain unknown. It is ruinous. To publish my refusal of it as an example to Colonel Washington or the Pennsylvania Farmer would be madness. In the first place, I am absolutely confident they need no such example. The Colonel is a soldier and a Virginian—a planter. I am sure that no persuasions would take such a man from his elegant country seat and his decent pursuits, to the council chambers at Westminster. The Pennsylvania Farmer is all for magnanimity, yes. But I do not believe for an instant that Mr. Dickinson's magnanimity could stretch to embrace this bribe—even if he should honestly believe that it were offered as a sober measure to carry out a noble 'healing' policy."

150

Abigail sat down now in the chair her husband had placed there for himself earlier. Settling herself with deft smoothings of her silk dress, she looked up at him. "Your confidence that those gentlemen of the more favored provinces would reject the proposal does you and them honor, John. I am glad to hear it. But I am convinced that even if it must remain unknown, your example is crucial. The honor of the colonies is safer as the result of your action."

He was a little crisp. "You exaggerate my importance, Abigail."

"Lord Hemynge does not," she asserted calmly. "He has not submitted the proposal to you by chance—nor at the prompting of fancy or whim."

This really gave John Adams pause. It was true. The "fawning courtier" had used terms that were repulsive to him because of the perfumes of flattery that wafted about them. But the creature had come armed with that opinion of Mansfield's. There was nothing fanciful or whimsical in William Murray's legal speculations. (By heaven, what an intellect, what a roomy chamber for cerebration there was in *that* hard Scotsman's head!) How sound his reasoning, in every department of state business, of great affairs—except, of course, in colonial policy, where he had a fatal blind spot. But even to recall his brilliant disquisition on the Scottish peerages upon the accession of the Stuarts and the later disposition of them by the Act of Union in Queen Anne's time, gigantically foolish as it was in application to Massachusetts Bay, was enough right now to put John Adams into an unexpected good humor. And with this turn of his spirits, he was able to accept his wife's implication that the Earl of Hemynge had given due weight to his, the Boston lawyer's, plea for the accused in the Superior Court of Judicature, Court of Assize and General Gaol Delivery, only two days ago. The state of his fatigues and his anxieties had prevented his taking the satisfaction any man should be entitled to in having done a task—in this case a very difficult and dangerous task—better than he had hoped. For the first time, it occurred

151

to John Adams that his success in that pleading was something that he could do more than survive. He had undertaken that defense as an act of rectitude approved by his private and his professional conscience, which were one. He or any man was entitled to a sense of pride in such an undertaking. Secretly, at this moment, he experienced a first pulsing of elation. For he had had, in the end, a triumph, and an envoy from the government had witnessed it—had, in fact, found it so noticeable that it had moved him to these pressing overtures.

He was determined not to admit to his wife that he was melting. He sat down in the settle and, striving to maintain his aspect of unapproachable dignity, challenged her. "Come, Abigail—it seems to me that you are exerting persuasions against me. I do not understand to what end. Give me what is in your mind."

Now Abigail knew that she had brought him around. "It may be that I am trifling in a grave matter that concerns only you and the envoy of the ministry," she said. "My only excuse, John, is that he spoke of it courteously to me also, in private, as though to submit the prospect before us to *my* view, as well as to yours. This is my thought, John. Lord Hemynge is a gentleman. And not in manners and graces only. He and his party mean well by us. Their proposal—while it is repulsive to you, and derives from a gross error in their understanding of conditions in the Massachusetts—is made in good faith. At least, *I* am forced to believe so. Perhaps you cannot agree to that."

She was appealing to him very directly now. "But John, whatever you think about the motives that have inspired this measure, I ask you to set forth your rejection of it in the terms of courtesy. Such terms can be clear and firm and decisive. Lord Hemynge has placed a proper value on your capacity to serve the British Empire in London, as well as in Boston. I know he is right in that, John. He is wrong in supposing that what he offers could be seen as an honor, by you. Tell him so, John, honestly—but without the 'heat' and 'disgust' that must make the failure of his mission altogether bitter. I dread that he

152

should report to Lord Chatham his meeting with Boston's man of greatest capacity in terms of resentment and—bitterness. By a courteous response, even though it is a complete rejection, you can provide against his doing so."

John Adams spoke only after a deep silence.

"You voice a respect for the character of this envoy that I have not been prepared to feel, Abigail. Perhaps if I were in better health and spirits I could have seen something more of merit in the man. I am forced to respect your judgment in this matter."

Abigail was almost ready to face a remorse that she had suggested an expression from her husband of a greater agreeableness or amiability than he actually felt toward any man's person and purpose. But he was not conceding all, not quite yet.

"What nearly overthrows my reason, Abigail, is that they pass over the willing Tories, Hutchinson and Oliver and their crew, and come to us—to me."

Once more she had to resist, and it was easy for her.

"But John, my dearest friend—exactly in that is their greatest show of sagacity!"

At last he caught her sense, and was amazed. He had never before been so dense in tracing a motive. But after all, he had never before dealt in direct negotiation with a seasoned emissary from the parliamentary ministry. The royal governors were different—they were fair bait for the whole General Court. But not so this peer, armed in his mission with the authority and approval of Chatham, Burke, Mansfield, Rockingham—even of His Majesty and the unspeakable Lord Bute. Abigail was right. It was immense, it was a brilliant stroke, it was a coup, it was a glimpse of the high audacity that inhabited the world of great affairs—and it was also a mad folly!

John Adams, lawyer, of Boston, member of the Boston seat, farmer of Braintree acres on the side, sat at his hearthside with Abigail, his Portia. He was suddenly liberated from an anxious burden. He realized that he had *not* been insulted. He felt that he might know again a recurrence of health and good spirits,

153

he was grateful to his wife, and delighted with her wit. He did his best to say so.

"By heaven, Abigail, what you say is just! This is all to the good. I shall talk to Lord Hemynge tomorrow at noon. And I promise you I'll give him no provocation to a duel."

⌘

John Adams slept well that night, better than for many weeks. The surprising debate with his wife had of course only furnished an opportunity for him to confirm in words the immediate, the unalterable decision he had necessarily made with respect to the proposal conveyed to him by Lord North's envoy. But Abigail's pretty reasoning had demonstrated to him that his announcement of that inevitable decision need not be couched in the terms of contentiousness. A simple dismissal would be amply effective—would have perhaps greater effect upon the envoy's mind than one expressed with "heat" and "disgust."

Nothing had contributed more to the result of calming Mr. Adams' temper than his own pleasantry on the subject of dueling. New England had had so little experience of actions ruled by the *Code* that his own unexpected mention seemed to him extravagantly absurd. He had no idea whether occasions that required the granting of "satisfaction" would have been usual to any extent in the life of such a nobleman as the Earl of Hemynge. But the fantastic image suggested by his reference: of himself and the peer standing back to back, pacing off eight, turning with rigid nicety, awaiting the cue from some cloaked and muffled second, then raising pistols to shoot at each other— or into the air, as it was reported to be done on some occasions —no, in truth, it was enough to make a man of sense laugh long and loud. It took a demagogue like John Wilkes to get himself involved in such kind of brawling.

Idle fancies were not familiar habitants of John Adams' mind, and if he were not so fatigued he might make the effort to check these, and even to chide himself for indulging in them.

154

But tonight they put him to sleep, almost chuckling into the counterpane.

But for Abigail Adams, this night was long and so was her lone vigil at the fireside. For one thing, to have entered and perhaps won a debate with her beloved friend was in itself a disturbing experience. And for another, to realize that she had concurred—without long and serious reflection—in what seemed to her now her husband's *hasty* decision with respect to the offer of a peerage, inspired uneasy doubt. Of course, John was being true to himself, as he had been when with equal swiftness and assurance he had rejected the offer of place from Sir Francis Bernard, the Royal Governor. But this—this was different. It did not emanate from one of those despicable characters, the royal governors. It came straight from the ministry in London. It was borne by an envoy who appeared to Mrs. Adams a person of capacity and quality. Her husband, too, was a man of capacity and quality—more, of genius. He would never, she felt, get as much honor as he deserved, in Boston. And here he was sought for what would be not merely high place in London, but in the British Empire, and so in the great world. In that place, his gifts would be noticed and admired of all men. If the splendid Lord Chatham had difficulty in finding men virtuous enough to support his noble views, policies, and measures, how greatly must he gain by having at his side, John Adams, Earl of Braintree!

The Bostonians—led by Sam Adams, of course—would be bitterly hostile, resentful to the point of violence, at first. But in the end they must acknowledge the advantage of having a truly sensible advocate in the Parliament at Westminster, and one who in *fact*—not "virtually"—represented them.

She began to wonder if it were not John's *duty* to accept this offer of elevation to a place of high responsibility.

How unwell she felt. Was she raising a fever?

Sam Adams—Sam Adams! He was the cause of so much of their discomfiture, and she recognized now that it was the thought of him that had heightened her agitation. Dwelling on his devious ways, for the moment, she was astonished once again that this strange kinsman had found it in himself to praise John Adams for undertaking the defense of the British soldiers in the late trial. Why? When he had so plainly desired them to be found guilty, and to be sentenced to hang by the neck, or to die before the firing squad. She stirred in revulsion —and bitterly thought it sure that Sam Adams had long ago foreseen that such an overture as the present one from London must come some day to John Adams—and so, carefully, quietly, subtly, he had secured and retained a hold on his younger cousin's conscience. He wished to make certain that John Adams would never act openly for the accomplishment of a peaceful settlement of the bitter issues dividing London and Boston, Old England and New.

Plainly, it was *her* duty now to awaken John and warn him against the insinuations and seductions of his palsied kinsman.

But suddenly she remembered the time when Sam Adams was a guest in the house, and little John Quincy had run to him happily, babbling about the "pretty redcoats." The soldiers even then were at their drill out in the square, and she had seen how the design forming in the visitor's mind changed the expression on his face. Without consulting her or John, Sam Adams had taken their little boy affectionately into his arms, walked out of the house with him, set him down upon the pavement, strolled along beside him, holding his trusting little hand. "No, Johnny—they are *bad* soldiers. *Not* 'pretty redcoats.' They are *bad* soldiers. *Not* 'pretty redcoats' . . ." over and over again.

She would never forget it. It had been a lesson to her, too. The man was an Adams, and worthy of the name. John held him in great affection, had a sturdy loyalty to him, honored him still when they disagreed. Let her never forget John's courage to disagree wherever he must. Oh, her husband, her husband! His honesty and goodness were become his wife's despair—for once.

For now, once again, she must join him in a view that she had long resisted inwardly: his view of Sam Adams' merit. Abigail recalled with a sudden vividness what all of Boston knew: that it was Sam Adams who in the night of March the fifth and the morning of March the sixth had spoken for the town—the town ready with fervor to back his every word, once it was spoken. Sam had spoken what all Boston in unison demanded: the removal to Castle William of "both regiments or none!" The rightness, the greatness of that demand overwhelmed Abigail Adams now. Sam and the town together had forced upon the helpless Thomas Hutchinson, the hapless Colonel Dalrymple, the *only* measure that could have conserved the peace in those hours and days after the bloody wicked work in King Street!

John had understood—he must have seen it instantly. And it was in fact that very removal of the soldiers from the town to confinement in the island fortress that had made it possible for her husband to undertake the defense of the accused—to give his own great proof that Boston could dispense justice even in her year of turmoil and agony.

Always she had been proud of her alliance with John Adams. Now it spread—forcing a long sigh of emotion from her: she was proud of her alliance with the Adams cousinhood!

The fire was low again. She was chilled, fatigued, shaken. She rose, moved to retire.

There was a picture floating somewhere—upon the counterpane, or against her closed eyelids, or simply in the darkness?—of a broad lawn spread before a modest white Palladian mansion. Two ladies sat in the shade of a noble oak, drinking tea that had been shipped from India. (No nonimportation agreement prevailed.) Were they the Countess of Chatham and the Countess of Braintree? Was the talk of silks, ribbands, bonnets, or philosophy? Or was the talk of their husbands! And that gentle sound of a shepherd's pipe, pervasive in the summer air—was it a strain of Mr. Handel's music performed by a small band of players sent over for the day by the Earl of Hemynge to entertain the ladies? And the children, mingling happily in games of Cicero and the Indians—were they all little Pitts and little Adamses?

It is possible to sigh yet once again and to fall into sleep, as a picture that has perhaps existed, but only once in a dark winter's night—that has perhaps existed, but only for a fleeting instant of the beholder's lapse into slight womanish weakness— fades away forever. And this possibility was realized exactly so, for Abigail Adams.

9

THE EARL OF HEMYNGE APPROACHED THE ADAMS RESIDENCE in Brattle Square at noon the next day with a serene confidence that his business in Boston was nearing successful completion. He certainly had read no portents in the behavior of his guests in the Province House the previous evening. Of course their hasty leave-taking might have been seen as slightly irregular. But so was most of Chatham's behavior irregular. Hesitations, playings for time, seeming moves toward rejection when acceptance of a proposal was intended, were common practices among leaders of the Lords and Commons. Tetchy health, until a gentleman's constitution should be eased by a relieving gout, was another commonplace. The peer took it as perfectly natural that Mr. Adams should be subject to some such complaint. The ability of a lady to take command of her husband's situation when he was distempered had been amply demonstrated in the past by Hester Grenville Pitt. That Mrs. Adams should show similar energy and concern in a less pressing difficulty of her own husband's contributed materially to enhance his lordship's already high opinion of this excellent colonial lady.

In the street, he directed the coachman to hold his carriage in readiness near by. He expected that he would not be over an hour in executing his business.

Mr. Adams himself opened the door to admit his visitor,

relieved him of his hat and his cloak, and led him at once to the same modest parlor in which they had first made mutual acquaintance two days earlier.

The peer inquired after the lawyer's health. Mr. Adams assured him that his indisposition had been transitory. He invited his visitor to be seated and then turned abruptly to the business in hand.

"I must tell you at once, my lord, that it is utterly impossible for me to think of accepting such a proposal as you tendered to me yesterday. A handful of peers in the House of Lords could never represent America, and if they were to be appointed to sit there for any purpose whatsoever, I could not consent to be one of them. The temper of the people of Massachusetts Bay is such that they would violently repudiate any fellow countryman elevated to high rank who pretended to speak for them in the House of Lords. I share that temper. If the question of colonial representation in Commons is to be raised, it must be submitted openly to our legislatures. There would be an almost universal opposition among our countrymen here to any passing over of those assemblies. I should approve such an opposition. For my own self, I must express my thanks to you for the honor implied in your submission of such a proposal to me."

Lord Hemynge's discipline was equal to the challenge of concealing the shock he felt on hearing this communication. He took in the sense of it clearly enough. He was forced to the recognition that he had been engaged in a wild goose chase: for it was impossible to suppose that Mr. Adams did not mean what he said. He had established his right to be credited absolutely. If the peer needed time, and he was not at all certain that he did, it was to be gained only by engaging now in an exchange of formal courtesies to cover his retreat.

"Such capacity as yours, sir, which I have myself seen proved, merits the *substance* of honor itself, not merely the *shadow* of 'implied' honor." He bowed, and went on to administer a mild reproof which, he knew, Mr. Adams might not recognize as such. "What has been submitted in this instance was intended to be the substance, not the shadow."

Mr. Adams recognized that he was thus invited to express something of confidence in the good faith in which the honors had been offered. He set his jaw a little more firmly, and determined to say nothing in that vein.

Lord Hemynge would give him another opening. "It is naturally of concern to me, Mr. Adams, to be informed whether it is the *terms* alone, or the *object* also of the present proposal, that produces this—dissatisfaction?"

John Adams knew that the object of the proposal was not merely that he, the Boston lawyer, should sit in the House of Lords. But he was not certain what was meant. "The object, sir?" he asked.

"Yes," said his lordship. "The object, of course, being a peaceful and just settlement of the issues between England and her North American colonies—which is to say, between the Parliament and the colonial legislatures."

Mr. Adams was not disposed to discuss such a question with an envoy of Lord North's ministry. But he decided that he could properly venture an answer to Lord Hemynge's inquiry. "I must of course respect such an object, my lord," he said. "But I should consider that it was being seriously pursued only if the troops were to be removed from Boston, from Massachusetts Bay altogether—and if the Parliament were to repeal those declaratory acts and tax duties that are regarded as oppressive by the people in these colonies."

"It would doubtless be the privilege, perhaps the obligation, of North American representatives in the Parliament to move for such measures," Lord Hemynge reminded him.

"Such persons would be unwise to deceive themselves that their weight would be very great in the Councils at Westminster," Mr. Adams responded with a touch of asperity.

Lord Hemynge smiled. He had been foolish to suppose that

161

even the men of greatest capacity in these remote provinces might be free of a sense of timidity on facing the prospect of membership in the most ancient of Parliaments.

"Your voice could make itself heard in any chamber, sir," he said lightly. "But only if you chose to raise it, of course. I must consider now, Mr. Adams, how I shall explain to Lord North and Lord Chatham this seemingly sudden collapse of the demand that has been so urgently raised from the Massachusetts for representation? We have always understood it to be a demand for representation in the British Parliament at Westminster. We have never understood that the colonies were agitating only for more of what they already have—that is, authority to legislate for themselves, and to *tax* themselves, in their own houses of burgesses, courts general, and the like. How may this be reconciled, Mr. Adams?"

Quite possibly here, John Adams recognized, there was an inconsistency, or the appearance of one, in the colonial position. Yet the slightly ironical tone used by the envoy of the government in raising the question moved the Braintree farmer to an even stronger sympathy than he usually felt with his countrymen's position, inconsistent or willful though it might appear to be.

"The 'demand' you cite, my lord," he stated, "was heard at its greatest intensity during the controversies that agitated Boston—and indeed all of our sister colonies—in the Stamp Act time, five years ago. Since then, there has been a falling off in the number of those who are firmly convinced that representation in the Parliament would be our salvation. It would not be that, of course. It may be our *right*—but that is a question that must be much debated among *us*, as well as among *you*, before a decision upon it could be reached. If representation at Westminster had been offered to us on an equitable basis five years ago, or earlier, we could hardly have rejected it. Today, many doubt that it would be 'practicable.' I believe you should find that the Sons of Liberty and the Acting Royal Governor think alike on this question, my lord—unfavorably."

"I am certain, Mr. Adams, that an examination of currents of opinion in various quarters of the North American bodies politic would produce many surprises for—His Majesty and his ministers," Lord Hemynge said dryly.

The scrutiny Mr. Adams had kept directed upon the peer's countenance during their conversation moved him now to a certain feeling of sadness. For he detected in the Earl's own manner traces of that very "levity" that had been described by this envoy himself, earlier in the negotiation, as "culpable." And yet—John Adams reminded himself—this man had been held worthy to sit in company with Chatham, Mansfield, and the rest; and he had impressed Abigail as a gentleman of capacity and quality. She had been pleased by his courtesy, had believed in his kindness, and had asked that courtesy and kindness be shown him in return. Her husband gave weight to his wife's opinion, as he did also to the fact that his visitor had been known in terms of respect to the greatest men of Westminster.

"There is no hope I should cherish more earnestly, my lord" —John Adams offered his best kindness and courtesy—"than the hope that the misunderstandings between Old England and New should be removed. I cannot tell you how that might be accomplished, sir. The remaining grounds for such hope, I fear, are of the slightest. Yet it appears that the valiant efforts of many honest men, working together, might yet effect such a result. Faith follows works, in state affairs. I do not know how else to put it."

Lord Hemynge warmed to his antagonist. He, too, felt that the great course of events that involved England and America was beyond comprehension in this colonial dwelling place, at least for the moment. He was moved to offer his own honesty, plain-spoken.

"The failure of my mission is indicated, Mr. Adams. It was designed to serve as part of such an effort toward the object we have been speaking of. My opinion is that this design must be reconsidered and amended by the ministry. I shall so report, and then I shall submit my resignation from my present appointment. I wish it to be understood by you that my *personal* hopes had become engaged in a favorable result here in Boston. I should have been most pleased to welcome you into the Lords."

Now the level of elegance maintained by the peer began to give John Adams a sense of uneasiness. If suitable for any capital, it was for Paris, not for Boston. "Your politeness is valued, my lord," he managed to say.

Lord Hemynge rose then, much to the relief of his host. "I may assure you, Mr. Adams, that insofar as I shall be able to keep it so, the nature of our conversation shall remain secret. Mr. Hutchinson has guessed that I am engaged in negotiation with you upon the subject of—honors. I should venture high, I think I may undertake to *guarantee* that *he* will maintain silence with respect to this subject."

John Adams enjoyed an instant penetration to his lordship's meaning. He allowed his expression nothing more than a trace of quizzical appreciation, however. The suggested image of Thomas Hutchinson coveting a peerage that was rejected by one whom he probably regarded as an insurrectionist, a subversive person, was not displeasing to one of the "brace of Adamses." To Lord Hemynge, he said merely, "I offer you *my* assurance that I shall speak to no one of this proposal, sir."

The two men still remained standing. John Adams felt a growing impatience that his visitor lingered.

"I find myself reluctant to take leave of Boston, Mr. Adams," the Earl of Hemynge said, "without the privilege of a word of farewell to your excellent lady. She is one of the finest ladies I have ever been privileged to meet."

John Adams made no move. "I shall repeat your compliment to her, sir," he said. Lord Hemynge found a brief entertainment in observing the discomfiture the colonial lawyer was suffering from the necessity to bandy courtesies at the close of this episode. He was glad that he had chanced upon the formula.

"If she is at home, and it should be convenient," his lord-ship obstinately pressed his host, "I should be grateful for the opportunity of a word with her now."

It was difficult to invent a pretext to put the persuasive man off. John Adams murmured, "At your disposal, I am sure," and left his visitor alone. He went to summon his wife.

In a very few moments Abigail entered the room, preceding her husband. "It is pleasing, Lord Hemynge, that this occasion permits me to thank you for the most agreeable entertainment you offered us yesterday." She was glad to see this visitor once more, and she spoke from her heart.

Lord Hemynge advanced to her, took her hand, saluted it, and addressed her warmly. "You are aware of what my purpose in Boston has been, Mrs. Adams. It was to discover a peer of the Massachusetts Bay. I have even exceeded my instructions and found for our society in London a lady perfectly endowed to carry the distinction of appearing there as the first North American peeress."

John Adams, standing just within the doorway, and stretch-ing his patience with the last resources of good grace wearing thin, was amazed by Abigail's easy manner of accepting such flattery, as though it were an honest and Bostonian mode of speech.

"Indeed, sir," she was saying to the Earl, "I wish that your mission required you to remain longer in Boston. And I should hope it might please you to give us further instruction in the delights of music, such as you have made us acquainted with so briefly."

"Perhaps that is a mission in which I could succeed," Lord Hemynge said a little recklessly. Then he went on very soberly: "But I am taking upon myself today a new mission, Mrs. Adams. It is, to work for the growth of better understanding between England and America." Mrs. Adams was sympathetic; Mr. Adams, whose feelings toward this visitor had been fluctuating from the first, was moved now toward respect.

165

"I pray that you may succeed in this honorable new mission, my lord," Abigail said simply. "And I hope that you shall not be lacking aid from these shores."

"I am grateful, ma'am," Lord Hemynge said. "And as I take my leave, permit me to tell you how deeply I regret that you are not to become Lord Braintree's Countess."

Abigail smiled and spoke gently: "Sir, it is quite enough for any woman to have become Mr. Adams' wife."

After the slight necessary flurry in which a polite departure was assisted and accomplished, the most disturbing visitor who had ever been received by Mr. and Mrs. Adams was gone, for the second and last time. Once again the master and mistress of the small house in Brattle Square stood together at their hearthside, each deeply aware of the other's honorable achievement. This time, there was nothing more for them to say to each other. They smiled: smiles that were perhaps a little grave, a little uncertain. When the sounds made by the passage of an uncommonly substantial carriage in the street just outside reached their ears, they did not even turn their heads.

10

The length of the voyage back to England, for Lord Hemynge, was determined not so much by the force and direction of the wind as by its perversity and unrelenting antagonism. The vessel again was H.M.S. *Cavalier*. While it was larger than the sloop in which Tompkins had crossed the ocean westbound, according to him it "foundered worse."

Lord Hemynge was at first amused by the extravagant expression of poor Tom's acute miseries, and did his best to tend to the prostrated creature with a reasonably sympathetic forbearance. But when the storms east of Newfoundland promised to become yet more violent, he found that he was losing his patience. He presently determined to try drastic means of ending the apparently endless nuisances the fellow was capable of committing.

First, he administered large draughts of rum. These were entirely wasted. Then, by summoning into his soul a ruthlessness that he had not called upon for more than two decades, he had the shattered invalid brought up to the quarter-deck, and insisted that he stand there as though on watch, to get the wind in his face and down his throat. "That, at least," his lordship murmured to himself, thoroughly out of sorts. Tom was in fact so weak that he could stand only by clinging to the lines, and if they went slack he went slack with them.

In the end, by forcing himself grudgingly to take on a sort of specialized boatswain's role, the peer compelled Tom to perform a variety of hard physical tasks on deck. Tom's distaste for the work proved a counter-irritant of some effectiveness, and he began once again to gain some sustenance from what he managed to swallow. By the time the brig was passing through her third storm, Tompkins had attained a fair sea-footing, and was sharply contemptuous of the handful of passengers who remained greenly bedridden.

The truth was that Lord Hemynge was looking forward with distaste to facing Lord North upon his return, with a report on the result of his American mission. The failure was of a nature that made him feel somewhat of a fool, and no Humbird had been forced to suffer such a feeling for several centuries. (There was said to have been a Percevale Hummingbird who served for a season at the court of Henry Tudor, about 1505, as a music-making jester. The sixth Earl of Hemynge refused to acknowledge that the line of descent was direct, or even collateral, but his Countess, the Lady Dorothy, had found the legend both entrancing and credible.) Lord Hemynge felt that he should be preparing his story so that he might emerge from his prospectively humiliating interview with the Prime Minister with the least possible embarrassment and the broadest possible credit. But the obligation bored him, and he found it difficult to give his mind to any intention save the resolve he had formed to retire altogether from public business.

It was the first of March before the peer and his still feeble secretary unpacked baggage at Hemmingcourt. His lordship rather grimly put Tompkins to work at copying out some scores from a collection of manuscripts attributed to William Byrd. After a day or two passed in sulky seclusion, he started out upon a week end to wait on the Minister at Wroxton.

On arrival there he discovered a large party in progress, with gaming at high stakes the major diversion. He asked the servant who admitted him to let him await the Minister's pleasure in a closet, as he did not wish to appear in company.

168

Lord North joined him presently in the small study. Lord Hemynge observed at once that the Minister had gained weight and lost confidence since their last meeting. If he still had the aspect of a good-natured man, it was mixed now with the aspect of an uneasy one.

"My dear friend," the Minister began, "I had no idea when we should see you again. But we scarcely expected it to be so soon. Have you had a tolerable passage?"

"It could not have been worse, in either direction," Lord Hemynge asserted with a candid petulance. "I no longer take to the sea as I did twenty years ago. I do not expect ever to set foot on deck again. I am harboring the sentiment that I was mistaken in doing so on this occasion."

Lord North made a chucking noise with his tongue. "It is a pity that you were sent out on such a voyage, since there was no need of it."

The Earl of Hemynge sat up. "No need of it, my lord?" he asked a little dangerously.

"You have had my apologies, of course," the Minister went on, "and now we have the news from Hutchinson. Apparently the ship he sent it by crossed more speedily than your own."

For a moment Lord Hemynge was conscious of an impulse to recross the Atlantic in the brig H.M.S. *Cavalier* so that he might assassinate Mr. Hutchinson. "He has broken the pledge of secrecy he gave me, and published the whole business? Do I understand you aright, my lord?"

Lord North looked at him with an air of mild surprise that his visitor was not following the sense of their conversation better. "Oh, no, sir, nothing of that sort. He makes no mention of your mission. He merely reports to Lord Hillsborough and myself that things are quiet in Boston since the end of that trial—of the soldiers accused after the business they called the 'massacre,' you know, a year ago?"

The impudence of Stingy Tommy, intercepting the Earl of Hemynge's own report to the ministry with a letter declaring "All's well in Boston"!

"So the Acting Governor reports Boston quiet, and no doubt penitent, and compliant?"

"Exactly so," the Minister confirmed his visitor's guess. "Most interesting, what he has to say—the chief smugglers are removing their 'law business' from the hands of the 'Patriot' men of law, and entrusting it now to respectable persons. The 'Liberty party' appears much broken and scattered as a result of the trial. He expects an early surrender from the General Court, and will restore it to Boston, at the first sign. I may disclose to you in confidence, my friend, that we are about to confirm him in the appointment as Royal Governor. He has earned it."

"The appointment will not be popular at Boston, my lord," Lord Hemynge commented.

"How should that matter, if the resistance of the rebel party is collapsed?" Lord North innocently inquired.

"Collapsed persons are commonly revived with salts, and so may collapsed parties be with spite, my dear sir," the Earl of Hemynge hazarded.

"Not with firmness on hand to keep them under," the Minister said sagely. "Hutchinson will do very well. He has been firm, and I doubt not he will continue to be. An admirable thing, really, to have one of their own men at the head, over there, determined to keep them in line."

But the prospects of "Honest" Tom Hutchinson at the "head" in Massachusetts Bay were not what Lord Hemynge had come to discuss with the King's First Minister.

"I do not quite follow you in the proposition that there was 'no need' of my making my late voyage, sir," he stated. He intended to be firm in steering a course away from the Hutchinson diversion.

"Oh, you had my letter on the altered policy," Lord North threw it off comfortably. "It might have reached you at Bristol if we'd been swift enough, but it must have found you at last in Boston?" He made it a casual inquiry.

"I have had no communication from the ministry, none whatsoever, since I took sail from England last October," the envoy declared.

Lord North opened his eyes. "Now isn't that devilish unfortunate, Hemynge?" The Minister appeared to be distressed by the inconvenience this mischance must have caused his old friend. Then, suddenly, a more alarming thought struck him. "God's mercy!" he exclaimed. "Don't tell me you've gone ahead and made an offer to one of the 'Patriots'!"

Lord Hemynge fixed him with an Admiralty-trained glare. "Do you mean to tell me—" He paused. He recalled that moody impression he had had on shipboard of having been made somehow to appear foolish. His memory did not flash back so far as to Colonel Dalrymple's outburst of fury in Mr. Hutchinson's house at Milton, but if it had his lordship would have recognized his own symptoms. Emotion of this sort rendered his voice very smooth and level in its tone. "Do you mean to tell me, my lord, that I have crossed that God-damned Atlantic ocean in midwinter on a fool's errand to Braintree?"

Lord North was not afraid of anger. He was not afraid of it in his Sovereign, perhaps because he never drew it there; and he was not at all afraid of it in his colleagues and subordinates, because he had learned that he could always manage magnificently both to aggravate and thwart it by a stubborn indecisiveness. What he *was* afraid of was the persuasive, badgering, almost loving pressure that was George the Third's great weapon against him, and that no one else had learned the trick of—and in fact never could, because no one else could wear the Crown of England, and no one else could refuse to accept Frederick North's resignation from the Treasury—which, after only one year as chief of the government, he was already more than willing to offer.

"'Braintree'?" he asked dully. "What's that? I remember nothing of a 'Braintree.'"

"It will be widely remembered," Lord Hemynge asserted with spleen, "as the landholding of the first North American commoner to be offered a seat in the House of Lords."

171

"Oh, no, Hemynge, it cannot be true. Surely you have not—" The Minister slumped in his chair.

"Yes, sir, I have—quite in accord with my instructions from the ministry," Lord Hemynge said sharply, vengefully enjoying the moment. "The earldom was offered to the most distinguished man of law, the most widely read scholar, the most handsomely wived husband, and the most eloquent orator of all, among the Sons of Liberty. A member of the Boston seat. One of the brace of Adamses."

Lord North was a shattered man. He covered his eyes with one hand, gave a limply nervous wave with the other. "Send for Lord Hillsborough. He will support me."

"Send for Dr. Franklin. He will support me!" Lord Hemynge retorted.

Even in his present collapse, Lord North could not miss the awfulness of this counter-proposal. He sat up again to look at his envoy. "Does *he* know?"

"Doesn't all of London—all of Europe?" Lord Hemynge demanded mercilessly. But the interview was going to his taste now. His cold anger and sense of outrage, of indignity, were retreating. He was inflicting punishment where it seemed to belong, though he was still not certain of the reason why this was so. "And it is surely Dr. Franklin's business, as *agent* for the Commons of the Massachusetts Bay General Court, to be informed of the exchanges between this country and his principals."

Lord North sank again. Finally he was able to summon voice for what sounded a merely flustered note—in the face of apparent disaster. "Then we are lost," he muttered. "America is lost. If they think they are about to be allowed representation in the House of Lords . . . But the King simply won't have it. If it had not been for that fatal stipulation that the honors go to men of the 'Liberty party' " . . .

"I am wanting in information as to the royal disposition, my lord," the Earl of Hemynge said blandly. "Are you telling me that His Majesty *changed his mind* soon after I was on the high seas with authority to scatter peerages over half of 'Patriot' America?"

"It was Bute. I am sure it was Bute," Lord North murmured.

"But he has not been First Minister for all of eight years," Lord Hemynge made bold to say.

"There is no such thing as a 'first minister,'" Lord North moaned. "There is the minister who receives the seals of the Treasury in the closet, and there should be no other to-do or 'first' or 'prime' business about it."

Lord Hemynge recognized what was once thought of as Frederick North's reservation based in a most becoming modesty. He was tempted to say: "Lord Chatham and Sir Robert Walpole have thought differently, and have acted accordingly—don't you remember, my lord?" But the thought of Chatham deflected him. There was somebody to face with this reversal and retreat accomplished. H'm.

"And the *consents*, my lord—the support that was to be given to the policy by the opposition, and by Chatham? Have all those parties been informed of the negation of the policy?"

"Burke said he never liked it. He said it was best you should be recalled at once."

Lord Hemynge suddenly realized that he, in his turn, had never liked that Irish adventurer. "It might have interfered with his prospects of appointment as agent for the colony of New York," Edward Humbird declared.

"Yes," Lord North groaned, apparently sympathetic to Mr. Burke in such an harassing situation. "It might have done."

Lord Hemynge suddenly felt a certain relief that John Adams was not to be set down in such a boggy political landscape as this. The ground at Boston seemed in comparison firm, untainted, and well drained.

"It is as I have said, my lord," he began sagely. "The offer of elevation to the peerage has been made to one of His Majesty's subjects in Massachusetts Bay. And it has been refused."

"What?" cried Lord North, with a resurgent hopefulness.

"Yes, Mr. Adams has refused the honors. Politely and firmly

173

he has refused the proposal that should have made him Earl of Braintree."

"Oh, I gather the point of your reference now. 'Braintree'—*Earl* of Braintree. Some country seat near Boston, perhaps?"

"That is it, sir, precisely," Lord Hemynge confirmed him.

But Lord North was thoughtful. "So he refused the honors."

"He refused me, and he would have refused the Prime Minister or the King," Lord Hemynge stated. "I must insist to you, sir, that his deserts are very great. Whatever the government's policy, it owes a considerable reward to the man who defended the soldiers as admirably and *successfully* as Mr. Adams did in that trial at Boston."

"That 'massacre' affair again," Lord North muttered with a trace of impatience. "You say this fellow was the one who served as defense counsel for the soldiers. I must say, Hemynge, that puts a better light on the business. I mistook you to mean that you had made the offer of the peerage to the other one— the master of the 'Sam Adams Regiments'—quite the rebel, I fear. Bernard proposes hanging, you know, for that one."

"Hutchinson may well end up proposing the same thing," Lord Hemynge said. "But to tell you the truth, sir, the thought of making the offer in that direction entered my head no more than it would have entered yours or Governor Bernard's." He paused. "But if it had, my lord," he went on, "I might have done as well as I did."

With that the Earl of Hemynge broke off. He recognized that Lord North could not understand what he was talking about. To carry on his mockery would do him no good, nor the Minister, either. He rose, determined to take his leave of Wroxton and of ambassadorial missions, forever. But he stopped for another expression.

"One more point, my lord—I may assure you that publication of the affair will never come from Mr. Adams. I do not expect it to come from Mr. Hutchinson, either. If it gets about, it will be from some of London's leaky mouths."

The Minister rose to speed the envoy's departure. "I do not

believe that it has been bruited about here, Hemynge." His tone was that of a party unjustly accused.

Lord Hemynge turned to him at the door. "Is Lord Chatham aware of this—ah, *revision* of the policy designed to 'conciliate' America, sir?" he asked.

"I really do not know," Lord North said, with his air of injury fattening upon him. "I daresay Burke may have informed him."

"Yes," Lord Hemynge said easily. "One dares to say that he may have done." Actually, he thought it very unlikely.

He left the Minister and Wroxton with a pinched feeling about his nostrils.

But the situation with respect to Lord Chatham worried him. In his carriage on the road to Hemmingcourt, he thought about his promise to wait upon the great man on his return from America. His inclination now was to join Lord North in the universal let-slide policy. Surely Chatham must have forgotten their interview by this time. In some odd moment at Hayes, perhaps, a recollection of it might visit him as a passing thought. If he should hear someone mention that Hemynge was now returned from North America, he might wonder idly how that proposed negotiation at Boston had prospered. But if the matter remained obscure, William Pitt surely would not trouble himself to the extent of *sending* to *remind* the envoy that *he*, Chatham, had expressed the desire for a report of the action taken at Boston.

The Earl of Hemynge convinced himself that the business would bury itself. As its appointed commissioner, he would press a report of it on no man, least of all on the Earl of Chatham.

11

SEVERAL WEEKS LATER LORD HEMYNGE MOVED ON TO LONDON.
Tompkins had gone ahead to open Humbird House in accordance with his lordship's instructions. The Earl had met little company since his return from America; and there were certain companies he was disinclined to meet at all—especially those that might include peers who sat regularly when the Parliament was in session.

But there came an April day so enchanting in its traditional English charms that the Humbird blood stirred from its lethargy. Tompkins was told to order the chaise—his lordship would drive out for an airing in the Hyde Park.

The groves were deliciously bright in the sun. The infant leaves in every tree strove with one another to show all sides of their new greenness as the light winds invited them to flutter, wave, and even to dance. Lord Hemynge drove his horse at a saunter, and found himself so well disposed to the gay company filling the paths and avenues that he formed the design to arrange an entertainment, a masque, at Humbird House. Or should he have a smaller company in to give a hearing to these strange experiments for four fiddles that were coming out of Vienna, from some fellow named—oddly English, for one from that quarter—Hayden. Surely a mistake to abandon

the *concerto* form bequeathed by Mr. Handel. But these—
what did they call 'em—quattuors—quattuoren, quattuori?
Anyhow, they were curiously agreeable.

Then across the Serpentine he saw it—*the* chaise with the
boot affixed at the side, racing as it was said always to race.
Fortunately, it was moving in the opposite direction. Lord
Hemynge decided to leave the park by the shortest way and to
return to cover in Humbird House.

But he underestimated the skill of Lord Chatham's groom,
perched precariously behind and above the cab. Apparently
the fellow knew the crossways. The rapid beat of the hoofs
of the splendid bay mare from the stables of Hayes Place soon
was heard behind Lord Hemynge, unmistakably overtaking
him. The circle had been covered in jig time. His lordship
decided that the best tactic would be to allow the racer to pass.
The probability was that he had not been seen by the formidable chief passenger—the Chief Passenger of the United King-
dom in any conveyance he might enter, God bless him, Lord
Hemynge thought, hoping also to God that the great man
would pass by without recognizing his onetime adherent in
the Lords.

But Edward Humbird was to know another disappointment
on this occasion. The swift chaise drew alongside his own—
Ay, if he wanted to board me, I should throw him a line at this
moment, Lord Hemynge thought with keen pleasure as the
Erstwhile Commoner cried out in tones that set the leaves to
further trembling, "Rein her in, Sampson!"

There was a great stamping of hoofs, a set of curiously gentle
cries from the groom, and a windy chattering from the foam-
flecked muzzle of—what would her name be? Calcutta?

Across the narrow choppy water between the two light
vessels—so it seemed to the erstwhile Captain Humbird—came
the friendliest of hails: "Hemynge! My dear sir! Welcome home
to England!"

Ah, it was one of his great days. "You are kind, my lord," the

177

returned voyager responded. Lord Chatham was wearing furs, but even more warmly he was wearing his Olympian affability, his archangelic condescension. The Nose itself in such a mood of its owner's lost its craggy Alpine character, seemed to have been hewn from some friendly shore, such as the cliffs of Dover. And best of all, the foot was not in the boot!

"My good Hemynge, I have been impatient to hear your news of my friends in America," Lord Chatham said very distinctly, while there was murmur of delight and approval in the crowd that had begun not so much to gather about the chaises as to grow by stopping its progress on foot just at that point.

"The North Americans, my lord, await your arrival by the next vessel," Lord Hemynge found himself saying with an hideous gaiety. "Boston, New York, and Quebec will fight for your favors like the three goddesses over the Apple of Paris!" Edward Humbird despised his elaborate figure. But he was uncomfortable from the question: and besides, he suspected that Chatham would like something of the kind—today.

There was no doubt about it, he did. "Ah, my dear friend, you are a very full man. Do follow me to my lodging and drink tea with me in a quarter of an hour. I must hear something more current of your observations."

"Indeed, my lord—" The Earl of Hemynge tried for an instant to believe that he could plead another engagement, but saw at once that he could not. "This is unexpected and most agreeable. I shall be honored to join you."

That giant head was drawn again within the shelter of the chaise, and a final word was uttered in the tone of command: "To the Countess's apartments, Sampson—full speed!"

The light graceful craft raced off, as though, Lord Hemynge thought, she were towed by a flock of seahorses and dolphins, and must be pursued in vain by a laggard companion vessel that moved only by the force of breeze against canvas. He stirred, and his own chaise began to move in the direction of the Argyle Buildings.

From the strength of the tea, Lord Hemynge judged that it had been brewed in the Carnatic and transported over the tropic seas in giant casks. He found it very supporting under Lord Chatham's extraordinarily close questioning.

The two peers had been closeted for near on to two hours. The late envoy in this time was recounting to Lord Chatham all of the principal incidents of his journey that have been set forth earlier in this narrative.

Whenever Lord Hemynge showed an inclination to condense, to shorten his account by summing occurrences into a general conclusion, William Pitt pressed him back to his last point. It would be: "What of these Justices at the Superior Court? How did they conduct themselves?" or, "About the troops of the garrison, now, how did they take to this incarceration in an island fortress? I must say, this has the aspect almost of a *French* treatment, has it not, my dear Hemynge?" or, "Both of these cousins, you say, are of the Boston seat? That is, in the lower House, the Commons, of the General Court of the Colony? These terminologies, my dear sir, must be drawn out of the ancient Charters, from the time of Charles, and Cromwell. Is there, as reported, a predominating spawn of the Commonwealth in that province, should you say, Hemynge?" (How was he to answer that one, Lord Hemynge wondered!) or, "You were most kind, sir, to speak of me to the Colonel. But what a fatal mischance that ever he should have been there at all!" or, "You must come to us at Hayes Place, my dear friend, and report to the Countess what you say of this excellent colonial lady!"

Edward Humbird in all of his previous conversations with William Pitt had been given reason to share the general opinion that, as an eloquent person, this was a difficult man to interrupt. But today Mr. Pitt's visitor was primed with questions and was pumped for substance. Never had attention more inviting nor courteous been directed to any report it had been

179

Edward Humbird's privilege to submit in any quarter. This turn to the interview he had dreaded filled Lord Hemynge with an extraordinary happiness.

But always there must be something in the Chatham responses to surprise his visitor. Today, it was the sudden coolness that came over the great man when Lord Hemynge enlarged upon his impressions of John Adams' excellent capacity, and of that colonial lawyer's eloquence. There was a moment's softening of the giant mask at one reference, when Lord Chatham could not conceal a swelling of emotion: "He invoked the Plains of Abraham!" He concealed his face with his hands. Lord Hemynge, once more touched by awe, shared the sentiment of his beloved Giant, recognizing that the costly, oh, so costly plateau had been the scene of the victory that broke the Great Commoner's heart. For in winning that triumph for England and Mr. Pitt, the young, the brave, the gallant, the handsome General Wolfe had bled to his death!

Lord Hemynge, feeling that even he was close to tears in witnessing such a powerful memory take its hold on the Earl of Chatham, preserved a respectful silence till the great head was raised again, and the statesman could give his customary Olympian attention to the grave business of state.

He heard Lord Hemynge out, through the terms in which the envoy had submitted the proposal, to the refusal returned "politely and firmly" by John Adams.

"Politely and firmly?" Lord Chatham repeated. "After how long reflection?"

Lord Hemynge was rather disconcerted. "The fact is, my lord, he did not give me an answer at all on the occasion when I submitted the proposal to him in the Province House, where I was lodged. He became indisposed, apparently while reading the documents I had offered him—the opinion of Lord Mansfield—"

"Quite enough to indispose a man of the strongest stomach," Lord Chatham asserted with a touch of heat.

"There were other writings, as well, my lord. His good lady

urged that he discuss no further business at the moment, and an engagement was made so that I might wait upon them the next day. I proposed that myself, I believe."

"Very proper, very proper of you, Hemynge," Lord Chatham declared.

"But I am quite convinced, sir, that Mr. Adams needed no time for reflection. I am certain that if he had spoken out immediately when he had finished the reading of the despatches, he would have refused us as firmly as he did the next day."

Lord Chatham went so patently into a reflection of his own that his visitor kept silence till he should speak. Then, after a moment, he did speak: "I find it possible to suppose, Hemynge —this may be a passing whim of my own—that his rejection of the proposal might have been in terms that would have been offensive to the ministry, if he had spoken it immediately. But the night's reflection may have suggested to his mind the expediency of refusing the honors, as you put it, 'politely and firmly.' " The statesman dipped into his own pool of reflection again, briefly, and then went on: "The more reflection a man gives to such a proposal, the more is he able to perceive its merits."

Lord Hemynge suffered one of those mental gasps to which he was given at times, but tried to let no evidence of his slight shock appear. He was permitted to make no comment, a situation quite as he wished it. Lord Chatham resumed his questioning:

"In your judgment, my dear Hemynge, what were the main grounds of the man's refusal?"

"That—" Lord Hemynge began, "that his fellow countrymen would despise any Massachusetts Bay man who accepted elevation to a peerage. That no American, seated in the Lords, could be accepted in America as representing the people there. That Mr. Adams himself shared these sentiments. That no passing over of the colonial legislatures would be tolerable to the people of the colonies. That in truth, representation in the British Parliament is no longer desired with any warmth by a considerable party of the Liberty or Patriot persuasion—that it is, in fact, no longer held to be 'practicable.' The last great advocate of such representation appears to have been one James Otis who lately has suffered a decline in capacity and dignity."

"As you report to me their thoughts, Hemynge, I must take these people to be very sober, indeed."

"They are that, my lord. There is much in the character of Boston, as I briefly observed it, that could redound greatly to the credit of British institutions."

"The more so," declared Lord Chatham, "in that *over there* they preserve those institutions *uncorrupted*."

Lord Hemynge had a reservation. "Not altogether in pristine purity, my lord," he offered.

"No, no—that must be granted," William Pitt conceded. "But the men are not easily bought."

It was the turn of Lord Hemynge to require a moment's reflection. If his mission *must* be seen as an attempt to "buy" a New England conscience (which he was not willing to admit), then it might be said to have provided sure evidence that John Adams, one of the bravest spokesmen of that conscience, *was* "not easily bought." But if the proposition were in more general terms, then he must acknowledge that he did not believe that Sam Adams, or the Quincy cousinhood, no, nor even Mr. Hutchinson, could be easily bought, either. His own conclusion was something of a surprise to Lord Hemynge.

Now he was ready to face Lord Chatham. "I agree, my lord, that they are 'not easily bought.' But I know of no attempt that has been made to buy them." He added the last with a certain pride.

The Earl of Chatham looked at him for a long moment, with a grave expression. Then he smiled. "It is to your honor, my dear Hemynge, that you respect to the end the character of your mission." The magnanimous Pitt forbore to remind his visitor that at their last interview he had used the words: ". . . so handsome as to be irresistible! . . ."

"And what *is* the end of it, Hemynge?" Lord Chatham

pressed on. "Will there be a second attempt? You tell me *you* resign your commission, having failed. I amend that: having failed with honor."

Lord Hemynge allowed a shade of grimness to pass over his face before he smiled his thanks. "The policy is abandoned, my lord. The Governor reports that Boston is quiet, and the Patriot party much broken up as a result of the trial and verdict. The government here is satisfied. Permit me to confess to you that I am not."

The interview must end. Lord Hemynge rose, and his host moved with him toward the door. There William Pitt stopped his guest, holding him with a light touch upon his shoulder.

"There is much to consider in what you have reported, my good friend. I am grateful for your account—even though it leaves me troubled." The statesman gently took his hand from Edward Humbird's person, moved away a few steps, turned again to face him from a more advantageous distance. "I rejoice to hear of English subjects who care deeply enough for English liberties to resist the invasion of them, by any power whatsoever. I am pleased by your account of this liberty-loving man of Boston, of so rare capacity and eloquence. We could use him here; we need such allies in London even more than in Boston. Your man, evidently, is as incorruptible as I might have hoped in my most sanguine regard for America. But do you know, Hemynge"—and Lord Chatham looked very solemn indeed—"I find in this very incorruptibility a certain ground for alarm. Can we ever persuade or reconcile such people?"

Lord Chatham again moved back to his guest, once more rested his hand gently on Lord Hemynge's shoulder. "As for your honest John Adams," he said, so low that it was almost a hollow whisper, "I regard him as lost to us. It is certain, now, that he will leave the ranks of the merely liberty-loving men. He will become a fighter for freedom. He will become—*altogether dangerous!*"

Lord Hemynge's nerves responded in the fashion that warned him he had heard once again the right note. He tried

183

to deflect the sense of awe that touched him. From the arch of the door that he had opened for himself, he turned to suggest:

"Perhaps he is no more than an honest man?"

William Pitt stood immobile. He brooked no amendment to his summation: "Altogether dangerous," he insisted. "Altogether dangerous."